Lily
the
Tiller

Lily
the
Tiller

Deborah
McKinlay

IMPRESS
BOOKS

Published 2022 by Impress Books

13-14 Crook Business Centre, New Road, Crook, County Durham,
England, DL15 8QX

Printed in the United States of America

© Copyright Deborah McKinlay 2022

Cover design by Heike Schüssler

ISBN 978-1-7397250-0-6

For my family; far-flung and perennial.

Lily the Tiller grew up a nomad and had no education to speak of, but what she knew from flowers was wondersome.

CHAPTER ONE

S he watches a man, of medium height and mellow coloring, engaged in the making of something. Beside him on a long, low, stone wall there is a hammer, with a black rubber handle, and a scatter of nails. Also, a jar. It is the sort of jar that some people (who had lived differently from the way that Lily had lived) might have known in their childhoods, in their grannies' houses, to have contained buttons, or sweets. This one contained more nails.

The man was dressed mostly for the country, in corduroy trousers and a thick navy sweater with holes in the elbows, but his pink striped shirt spoke of somewhere else. As did his hold on the hammer when he lifted it, having removed another nail from the jar. He held the nail, with the thumb and index finger of his left hand against the non-compliant corners of a pair of right-angled pine planks, swung the hammer and let fly a brief string of curses. He had his thumb in his mouth when he noticed Lily.

Lily had left her van on the main road, walked to the turn-off along the narrow lane and up the steep curve of the driveway, stopping twice to look back down through the rhododendrons at the view. She liked to approach a house on foot; it was quieter, gave her the observer's advantage and offered the possibility of retreat in case her instincts had drawn her to the wrong one. Lily's instincts, taut as violin strings, had yet to fail her completely, but she had in some cases made mild misjudgements and Motthoe was an altogether different house from the houses she had approached before.

Motthoe was a mansion. A stately upended shoe-box, facing south over its own woodland and fields. Lily would have liked to have lifted it and twisted it a quarter turn, toward the sea behind her – mirror-bright today, quivering in a soft breeze. The building was pinkish-beige, like a Golden Leaf-Edge orchid, except for the exposed north-western corner – blackened by two hundred years of elements – and the ivory columns of the portico. The windows, larger on the lower floors, smaller as the levels rose, shone in the morning sun that hit them now. It was the glint that gave the building its grandeur. Sunshine, if bright enough, works like bleach.

In fact, most of Motthoe was not nearly as grand as its

façade suggested and there were plenty of clues as to this state of affairs for the mildly keen observer. Lily was an extremely keen observer and took in straightaway a broken ceramic urn and an abandoned deck chair in a mass of crocuses – the chair's once-blue stripes now smoky with age, the white canvas yellowed and stained, one arm snapped into a crooked salute. The edges of the lawn were uneven and the centre was patchy with puddles and weeds – thriving, even in February, in the mild climate of south west England. More of them poked through the gravel at Lily's feet.

'A birdhouse,' the man said, waving his uninjured hand behind him, indicating the abandoned planks; explaining himself, as if he were the interloper, rather than she.

'Yes,' said Lily, as if she had known this right away, because a woman who is reliant on strangers for work, an itinerant, learns quickly to fit with people.

'For owls,' the man said.

Seeing him now, fully, from the front; a Silver Birch – mop-haired and romantically unformed around the jawline – Lily thought: forty, or thereabouts. 'Owls,' she said. 'Symbols of wisdom. And doom.'

'Doom,' he said. He lowered the thumb. 'I thought building something on a minor scale might be within my capabilities. I was wrong.'

It is a soft delivery, but Lily who sees all, knows all, detects in it the faint, sour mix of humiliation and annoyance. 'A seed-raised wisteria can take twenty years to bloom,' she said, 'Sometimes it takes time to find your gift.'

The words had their edges filed completely away by the dulcet burr of Lily's accent – accent of thick cream and ripe apples and sunsets. And Harry, Lord Harry of Dreams, romantic as mist, fell in love with her for saying them at the exact same time as he dismissed them as piffle. This is Harry's life – heart on one side, two hundred years of heritage on the other.

Lily, head and heart for the moment aligned, smiled and said, 'Lily the Tiller; gardens loved.' By way of introduction.

'Harry,' said Harry. 'Gardens neglected.' He smiled, too, in this open territory. 'As you see...' he finished, with a big, awkward swish of an arm.

It is the awkwardness that makes him so unthreatening – Lily is permanently alert to Threatening. He walked toward her.

'I do see,' she replies.

And Harry, although he is not always the most intuitive of fellows, can tell, or believes he can, that there is no judgement in this. 'Are you looking for work?'

Something in his tone, something beneath the apologetic politeness, firms up, suggesting to Lily that what he lacks in construction skills may be made up for by a certain amount of local clout based on nothing but birth. The Hopeless Son, she thinks. 'I am,' she says. She lowers her green, canvas backpack, sliding it from her shoulders with the grace of a flushed fawn clearing a brook, and smiles again – spring embodied. She is dressed in layers of colored wool and floral cotton. Her tan boots are laced up to meet the swinging hem of her full skirt. Her hair, a plaited, chocolate rope, spills around her neck. She flips it away.

Minnehaha, Harry thinks, *Poetical maid and legendary beauty*. 'All hands welcome,' he says.

'Got two.'

She held out her hands. They didn't look to be gardeners'

hands, but she said that they were and Harry wanted to believe her. To believe in her – Lily the Tiller. If you bury a wish long enough, maybe it sprouts.

If he liked, she said, she could look at the grounds and get the measure of things. They could discuss what needed doing. What she could do. Harry thought this a fine idea, so they walked.

It was February, twenty-ninth – Leap Year, day of rare magic – and a splendid morning, with sprinkles of frost still crisping the hollows. Lily – her turn for authority now – talked to Harry, as they progressed along the tiered section of garden at the front of the house, about his bedding and borders (all woeful neglected) in a tone of loving authority that Harry had not heard since the voice of his grandmother had stilled – darkest of dark days, 26th of June, 1982. The wrenching pain of that loss – particularly cruel for a motherless child – had been later moderated, but it was recalled again now, briefly, by the musical tongue and unparalleled knowledge of Lily the Tiller. She could see underground. And into the past. Through the leaf muck and brambles, all the way to the lost hellebores.

'They're there,' she said, 'but suffering a dire lack of encouragement.'

'Yes,' said Harry. Harry could see how such a thing could happen. He asked Lily if she would be willing to be the pathfinder; the seeker and discoverer of the buried floral Shangri-La.

She said she would. And outlined her terms. None to speak of, but she advised him that Interference tended to cramp progress. (None Forthcoming, Harry promised). And some assistance would be required with the heavier labour. (Offered). Additionally, she, Lily, even on longer, thornier projects – such as Motthoe would likely be (Affirming Nods) – never slept in the houses she gardened: A Policy – no matter the number of rooms, any one hers for the choosing in this case.

Harry, whose Owl House had been the shiniest prospect for his day before Lily's arrival, took in the possibility that she – divine interrupter of failure and aimlessness (Harry had plans, but they were often as hard to find as the ends of tangled wool) – might stay a while. It was a possibility that he was brimming to solidify. He looked down at Lily's boots and asked if she was up to crossing a field. Lily did not answer, but smiled in a way that indicated that she was up to crossing the Sahara should the need arise.

They entered the field – which sloped steeply upwards, over and down again like a disturbed counterpane – by rounding the east side of the house, and followed the hedge line to the end where, on a corner plot, flanked on one side by a driveway (leading to Motthoe's disused stable block and still-used garage) and on the other by a single-track country lane, there was a cottage. A sign on the cottage gate said ASHCOTT, but the lettering of the A and the S had worn off.

The cottage was furnished, low-ceilinged, mullion windowed, charming, and tangy with damp. It was currently home to a family of field mice, a lace web spider and a small bat. There was a house martin's nest in the porch. Harry said that Lily could stay there if she wished. Lily said that she would. Harry, although he'd let himself hope, was astounded. Harry could dream, but he lacked vision.

On the day that he had returned to Motthoe, not a year before – the day before his father's funeral – Harry had, like Lily, left his car at the bottom of the hill and walked up the driveway. He, too, had wanted to arrive in silence. In his case to gain time, to absorb his own entrance. He had wanted the trees to soothe his first sight of masonry – the pilasters and the parapets that were now his. Every upward step of that walk, of that day, had felt harder to Harry, as if the air itself were becoming heavier. It was late August, late evening and hot. Hotter than Spain, hotter than Italy, hotter than France, the car radio had informed him. Harry had left France twelve hours earlier; taken the ferry, driven the featureless highways from the port. It had been one of those journeys on which nothing is noticed, but a great deal is remembered for ever.

Harry had got himself installed at Motthoe – in an oak-paneled suite with an inefficient bathroom and a westerly vista – and friends (of the sort that a person collects in the course of ten peripatetic years) had come, and their friends. They had eaten cobbled-together meals and slept on cobbled-together bed linen and made cobbled-together go-karts, and roared them around the lawns and the largest of the barren halls. Most had arrived empty-handed, and many without introduction, and several had left with trinket mementos – inkwells, glasses, paperweights, soap dishes, cruet sets and, once, a pair of ornate limestone finials.

But the weekends had grown quiet after cold's first bite. Motthoe's heating was, at best, unreliable and by October fifteenth the pitiful plink of water hitting buckets echoed through the empty halls, and draughts whistled under every door. The effort of placing foot to freezing floor from bed or bath demanded pioneer grit, and the faintest exhalation of morning breath turned immediately to a pea soup pall. Rats, seeking winter quarters began to walk boldly along the deserted, rear passages.

Against this fade of the partying weekenders, a whey-visaged, strawberry-blonde (on the run from her thirties and the too-frequent weddings of her friends) had hung on, and kept Harry warm for a while. Her name was Tish. Tish, by way of making herself indispensable, had suggested Bed and Breakfast at Motthoe. There were masses of people, she assured Harry, in the market for History with their eggs and bacon. We could give them tours, Harry, she said… and alpacas. Tish had headed purposefully for the second floor, hauling a large bolt of toile de jouy and a glue gun.

Harry had gone along with Tish's notions at first, ignoring the unpalatable prospect of a Gift Shoppe – full of hand-crafted tat and cheaply printed postcards – but by Christmas the enthusiasm wrought by Tish's long thighs, and what had seemed at first like her companionable chatter, had waned. The thing dead-ended fairly quickly after that, with a Boxing Day farewell that was wounded on her part and relieved on his. Since then, there'd been nothing long-term for Harry in the feminine company line, unless you counted the infinite adoration of Loyal Irene. Harry didn't.

When Irene caught rear sight of Lily – morning number one of Lily's residence, March 1st – fixing a festoon of bunting across the hitherto gloom of the front porch of the back valley cottage, she felt the torment begin to churn in her. It was worse when Lily turned at the sound of the car engine cutting and her plait flipped across her cheek.

Good Lord, Irene thought, *Minnehaha*.

Irene had pulled over because she had spotted activity at Ashcott on her rounds. Irene did her rounds on her way to work in the mornings; drove off the link road, wound through a tiny village (twelve houses, an ancient church and a good pub), and then bumped her serviceable saloon along a narrow track that was only ever used otherwise by farm vehicles. She skimmed the outskirts of the estate, noting fallen trees, and dead badgers, and swollen streams, and straying sheep, until she came in eventually by the back entrance. She considered this one of her duties, though it had never been asked of her. Irene took her duties at Motthoe very seriously.

'Hello?' she said, at Ashcott's gate, sounding querulous, half hoping that the mirage would dissolve.

'Hello,' said the mirage, real as an anvil, though marshmallow in texture. She was wearing a blouse, Irene noted, that was far too insubstantial for spring.

Irene, unfairly flustered on her own turf, tried to summon Command, though she had no natural bent for it. In the absence of a miracle that bestowed exquisite comeliness, however, she figured it her best shot. 'You are…?' she said.

Lily lowered her bunting and gazed at Irene and saw there: Unrequited Love, glaring as a dandelion in a rose patch. 'I am Lily,' she said. 'Gardens.'

Well, Irene told herself – ever on the hunt for the workable feature – a Label would help. Something to hide her pride behind when folk pointed out, as folk were wont to do – down the local (skittles night, quiz night) round the Post Office cash register – that Squire Harry the Younger; idler, fantasizer, soft-haired, soft-handed, soft-headed, laid back, posh boy – had a new woman, a nymph, installed. 'She's there for the *Gardens,*' Irene would say, as if explaining all. And then she'd make her escape before the gossip and eye-rolling turned feverish.

'Irene,' said Irene. But nothing more, because what more was there?

Irene's affection for Harry (the secret light of her days) was, naturally, unacknowledged, especially by her. She knew that she fitted, in his mind and his talk, into a flat, undistinguished spot; below the Labradors, and above his dentist, but this was a position that she could settle in snugly enough, as long as nothing *unsettling* – with legs all long, up and under a florally skirt – materialised unannounced. 'I... help out...at Motthoe,' she said.

'Would you like some tea?' asked Lily.

This invitation was issued with such sunny directness that Irene found herself accepting it almost without thinking. And with it, her inevitable future of a Shattered Heart.

The milkless tea was pink and Irene didn't quite trust it, but it didn't taste as bad as it might have done, and, at Ashcott's kitchen table, she amused herself with the possibility – slight – that Harry might wonder why she was late. Lily did not sit with her, but continued in her blithe ebb and flow of organising and prettifying, though the room was already clean and congenial – the old coal range was lit and radiating low, even warmth. Irene felt a prick at the realisation that Harry had probably helped to bring the coal in – because that is the sort of effort that a prime set of breasts will elicit – but she was encouraged, nevertheless, by the order that Lily had imposed in such a short time.

The table and floor were cleared of dust and scum respectively, and the cottage's collection of mismatched china – slackly washed and poorly stacked by the last set of weekend guests – had been taken out from behind the sticking latched doors of the kitchen units and rinsed. They were draining at the sink's edge.

Irene found Lily's beauty less daunting now she'd seen it diluted by a practical streak. And she prayed that this practical streak was as wide as the Nile, because it was she who had borne the fallout of Tish's Bed & Breakfast fiasco: a minor ceiling collapse on a couple from Calsford. There is only (she had explained painstakingly to Tish, who had dragged these unhappy customers to the house from the car park of The Green Man) so much that a glue gun can do. Harry at that point had been still wearing his Lust Goggles, so Irene's words had gone mostly unheeded, but Tish had charted her own downfall soon enough, with her increasingly ambitious plans and her perpetually restless tongue. When, at last, Harry had come back to what wits he had where women were concerned and the bowed derrière of Tish's dolly hatchback had swung off down the driveway for the last time, Irene had watched its huffy departure with a distant sensation of lightness.

Lily, hoisting herself up to sit on the counter next to the

draining dishes, began to clean the windows above with a white cotton rag. The room filled with the sharp, enlivening aroma of vinegar. 'He doesn't live up there all alone, then?' she said.

'Oh, I don't live there...at Motthoe,' Irene answered, feeling, for some reason, embarrassed by Lily's assumption that she did.

'No?' Lily said, turning her liquid eyes to Irene for a moment.

'No. Dan does.'

'Dan?' Lily said. The interrogative was again unmatched by her body language, which exuded benign unconcern; a stream, slipping through a summer meadow.

'He's a friend of Harry's. Or, a friend of a friend of a friend of Harry's...' Irene put her cup down and watched the three-quarter angle of Lily's face. She's like a magazine cover, or a painting, Irene thought, made real. 'I forget the exact acquaintance. He's been living here since late last year. Not in the house exactly, in what used to be the driver's quarters, above the garage...Spends most of his time there, or wandering. Alone. You wouldn't call him sociable.'

Lily's smile came over her face in a slow trickle, warming as syrup. She finished her polishing and got down from the counter top with a pixie-nimble hop onto her bare feet.

Irene didn't want their chat to end. She was feeling listened to, which was novel. 'And The Gigglers,' she said.

Lily laughed at this, which was enormously encouraging.

'Two girls,' Irene went on, 'who've been tenants in the Nanny Flat since New Year. They work in the town, but they've shacked up out here for the peppercorn rent.

They bring boyfriends back on Friday nights – a selection. There's a fair bit of raucousness if you care to pay attention. Nobody does.'

Lily laughed again and Irene, all frothed up by this appreciating sound, accepted more of the pink tea. 'And there's a nice woman, Ruth, up here three weekday afternoons. She does her best to clean, but it's too much for one person. Her daughters come with her sometimes, in the school holidays. To help...'

Irene's face indicated her low rating of the Help offered by Ruth's daughters. She patted her hair. It was brown hair, beginning to gray, of the kind that turns into a wayward halo of fuzz at the first hint of humidity. Irene, in a life spent wedged between moor and ocean, could count the days when her hair had behaved (and the world had been entirely free of disappointment) on one hand. She gave up on her hair and unzipped her brown, padded gilet. Beneath it she was a nicely shaped woman who had undergone some sagging – the sort of sagging that besets a person when she has no cause to think about, or look at, her own body. And nobody else to do it for her. Irene could have been any age between forty-eight and fifty-three. She was forty-four.

'And the garden?' Lily asked.

'There's only a boy to do the grass, since Tim died. Tim was gardener to Harry's father – dreadful arthritis at the end. The grass boy comes weekly, mid-April to October. There's no one now for the flower beds other than the odd casual worker. Well, and you...'

'Lily the Tiller,' Lily said.

The tea was finished. The cleaning things were stowed.

Irene roused herself and stood with a slight, bustling scrape of her chair, and re-zipped her gilet. Lily walked with her out to her car. They stood together a moment at the gate. The sky was blue again. Above them a skylark sung.

'Welcome, Lily. Welcome to Motthoe – though it's not really my place to say it,' Irene said, humble as her white cotton knickers.

Lily's van had been advertised in the classifieds section of a small-town newspaper that had a photograph of the mayor and some children in animal costumes on the front page. She had bought it the way a person who is about to catch a train adds a packet of peppermints to their magazine at the station kiosk – without preamble. Lily bought all her vans this way, ditching one for scrap, taking on the new one, handing over cash in suburban driveways, or roadside lots. She had no attachment to her vehicles – she liked them to start, to go along, to be easy on petrol and to look anonymous. She kept her bedding in the van, and a warm coat and two hats – one straw, one felt. It transported compost, mulch, containers, and trees from time to time – tied to the roof or extending from the roped-open rear doors – but she kept her life in her backpack.

Lily finished emptying the backpack now in her cottage kitchen, laying the items on the table (once a card table, baize removed, requisitioned by a visiting flautist the previous summer and brought down from the main house on the shoulders of her lover), in a small ritual of stock-taking. She had already removed, the night before: her soap, her rosemary shampoo – she made it herself with jojoba oil – her toothbrush and a small tube of toothpaste. But there was left a skirt, twin to the one she was wearing (made for her by a woman in Loswithycombe, who had also made Lily two winter underskirts from recycled flannelette sheets), three sets of underwear, her spare long socks, a pair of flat sandals, two muslin blouses, a cable-knit cardigan – the color of clay – two pairs of leather gloves, a tin of beeswax hand-cream, and two black ballpoints. And her notebook.

On the cover of the notebook was its number – #57. Lily was twenty-eight and she had been keeping notebooks since she was seventeen (feint-lined, soft covered). On the first line of the first page of the first notebook she had written: *Primula Japonica,* and she had filled an average of 5.3 notebooks every year since – this was not mathematics that Lily could have done for herself. As a child, Lily had been on the wrong side of the lemony tongues of the sorts of teachers who place great emphasis on subtraction, spelling and penmanship, but Lily's notebooks and the scrawls and scribbles and sketches therein, the mass of collected facts and observations, were her best and most constant companions.

Lily read her notebooks to the exclusion of anything else, save the musty gardening books that she bought from market stalls from time to time, and sold the same way. Lily did not read newspapers. She did not know when there was a murder, or a fire, or an accident, or terrorist attack; she did not know that some poor family, distant and unknown, had lost a child, or a father. These were things that she did not want to know, did not want to bear. Lily knew the water requirements of astilbes, the effect of frost on oxalis, and the earliest and latest dates that cherry trees had blossomed in the northern hemisphere. She committed her own notes on these things to memory, learned them by heart in the writing and rereading. Often, she spoke portions of her notes out loud to herself – when she was setting out annuals, weeding, or spreading mulch – like mantras. Then, when she had filled a notebook and fully digested its contents, she chose its burial place – shredded its pages into appropriate compost, or burned it and put the ash on the soil of whatever garden she was working on. She left behind the dust of her studies for the worms.

Sometimes, if Lily was tempted to keep a notebook, if she found herself hesitating over the licking flames of a brushwood pyre, with the smell of smoke biting at the back of her throat, she pictured herself surrounded by the weight that other women were dragging through life: ornaments, place mats, sugar bowls, picnic jugs, empty vases and still-tagged dresses – belongings that blocked their way, and stuck them in their spots sure as concrete blocks tied at their middles might. She had no desire to be one of them, to be anchored by ownership, to be closed off from the possibility of escape. The possibility of escape was oxygen to Lily.

She refolded her clothes now and returned them to the back-pack. Then she sat and wrote in notebook #57: *Magnolia Campbelii*. She had seen one, in Motthoe's grounds the day before, in full flower, though it was still three weeks before the official start of spring.

Lily had as yet only toured the forward and eastern sides of Motthoe's gardens. After Harry had shown her to Ashcott the day before and led her through it (kicking at skirting boards, opening windows, testing the swing on doors) and, as Irene had supposed, brought the coal in with a big, old Made Fire look on his dial. After that he had left Lily alone – withdrawing with three, long, backward strides – to 'get herself settled.' And she had.

She had driven into the nearest town. It had taken her thirty-seven minutes. She had parked in the central carpark, found a store that sold everything she needed (lemons, baking soda, soft cloths, twine) bought them with cash and driven straight back. Lily wasn't much for towns, even the small, innocuous country ones, with their pedestrianized high streets and striped awnings, hanging baskets and quaint homeware stores, and proper greengrocers, reminded her of the underbellies of their unfriendly big sisters.

She had spent the rest of the day cleaning the cottage. But she had slept, as she always did, in her van, with the doors locked and the key in the ignition.

Now, Lily walked, via the back driveway that Irene had used an hour or so earlier, to Motthoe's rear entrance. Irene, seeing her arrival from the ground floor room that served as Harry's office – and was still lined with the metal filing cabinets that had lined it when his father had used it for the same purpose – put off a telephone call she had been intending to make to a plumber and went out to greet her.

As they made their way together, along the rear side, talking amiably, bonded in their morning's friendship, Harry spotted them from an upstairs window, where a brocade curtain the weight of two horses hung perilously from its fixings off one side. The sight saddened him as heavily as the curtain did its pole – Lily was already hijacked, no longer his alone. He raced down to lag lonesome behind the women.

Dan, the garage dweller, easing out from his upstairs apartment – his sleep under the beams, two dogs for company – sipped coffee from a chipped mug and watched the threesome silently over it, from a shaded spot on the garage wall. Two dogs watched him. Lily sent him a look from the back of her head. He shook it off.

'Where does this go?' Lily asked.

A path, near the kitchen entrance, led to a wall with a blue painted door. They went through it. Separated from the house by a strip of lawn and three, wide curved steps was a garden; an acre and a half area, just over, walled on two sides by faded red brick, and on the third by a yew hedge that straggled and curved to the right, hiding a small greenhouse from view. At the base of the garden, separate pathways led off into enclaves, and one into the woods beyond. This had originally been a kitchen garden, then a formal garden, then a more relaxed mix of cutting plants had crept in. After that the ivy and the ground elder and the bindweed and the brambles had taken over. Nettles, too, in great swathes at the woodland side. Of these, the bindweed, Lily knew, would be her greatest obstacle.

Twenty years, Lily guessed, the garden had slept there without any endeavour applied beyond scratchings. There were daffodils gone riotous, ivy on the rampage. Stone planters sat mossed; on its side, home to a toad. A totter of willow panels – evidence to more recent efforts – lay under a tarpaulin, in reasonable shape. Crampbark grew tall to wall height in the right-hand corner. Massed lavender had gone twiggy, with the rock roses. Euphorbia splattered its acid unchecked. Work to do, thought Lily, but, oh what fruits to bear.

Lily sat – in the manner of a silk thread dropping from a sewing table – on the second of the curved steps. Above them, to one side, was a paved area designed for a table and chairs, though it would have presented a major challenge to a spirit level. Harry and Irene, pleasantly afloat in Lily's wake sat down, too – Harry taking the top step and planting his feet casually and with unintended intimacy just to the left of Irene's bottom.

Harry and Irene listened and Lily spoke: she would take on One Garden. This one. One raggedy patch that she could bring back to something pretty and heart-lifting. Not perfection – that was a five-year task and longer. But she, Lily, would pass on all she could regarding its future development and care, before she left.

Harry, shutting from his mind any icy thought, that second clement morning, of Lily's departure, got a look on his face that was the kind of look that Tish's face had often borne – a pushing-through kind of look that denies all warning.

Lily, though, smiled. She had been honest and had promised nothing that she could not deliver – she never did. Her toes, bare still – Harry was delighted to note – stretched and arched towards the edge of the step below her. Alyssum, she was thinking, frilling along the rise, like sea-foam.

'You'll need Money?' Irene said. Because who else would it fall to, to confront the nitty-gritty?

Lily nodded, pulling her eyes back, treacle slow, from imagination.

And therein lies the problem, Irene's eyebrows signalled.

Harry was just about to bust forth with a blustery, over-promising, lacking-in-common-sense reply at which Irene would have bitten her lips, when Lily interrupted him. (Balm, she was, Lily.)

'We could raise some,' Lily said.

Harry and Irene were all ears.

'Terracotta seedling pots,' said Lily. 'They're popular for window ledges in false gardeners' kitchens. There's two hundred or more in the lean-to behind the stables. A few half-barrels, too – they'd do nicely for herb planters. And then, in the next few weeks you'll have daffs. We can sell those in bunches – at the weekend market in Falston. That should make enough for the immediate costs.'

Irene grinned at Lily and brushed brusquely at something non-existent on her beige gabardine trousers – pleated at the front and no favors behind – getting herself into the activity of it all, aligning herself with a fellow Doer.

Harry stared. Beauty and brains; Lily was too much for him.

'Saturday, then,' said Lily. And she rose. Morning over. Nuts and bolts in place.

Behind the wall, but within earshot, one of the Labradors, bored of nuzzling Dan's knees, yipped. Dan threw a stick and the dog lolloped off with its mate – older, beginning to whiten at the snout, but less distracted and straighter to the target. They tussled for it under an oak. Above them a squirrel startled and darted.

Harry looked up – the eye of his childhood and some of

its instincts not so removed – and noted that the creature, scampering along an oak branch that brushed the garden wall, was gray. His father would have shot it – over his son's head if need be. Grey squirrels; vermin who had seen off their red cousins and diseased the trees. *Boom*. Sometimes, Harry, boy untended, home briefly from school, would find the carcasses – no eating in them, left to putrescence. When he buried them, he recited whatever lines came first to mind over the disturbed soil – *'In that rich earth a richer dust concealed'* – with respectful solemnity. He left the graves unmarked. Only he knew the boneyards that peppered Motthoe's reaches.

Now, reluctantly wrested by mention of the plumber, and apparently dismissed by Lily, Harry got up and walked with Irene back to the house – leaving the goddess behind in her new dominion.

Dan, waiting, motioning for the stick to be dropped at his feet from the tenacious jaw in which it was clamped, decided that he didn't like much any of it. But that was Dan for you. Not a Liker.

Very late, after midnight, first quarter moon, Lily bent and undid the laces of her boots and removed them, and peeled her socks from her feet and set those aside, too. She walked two strides into the center of a messy sprawl of wild geraniums and burrowed her toes underneath the new growth. Twisting her feet left to right she bored down under, where the damp lived soft, and down more into the earth, forcing one foot, then the other, into the ground, deep as she could. Her legs set slightly apart, her arms V-crossed over her slender middle parts, she tipped her head back, eyes closed, and felt the powerful heart-pound of herself fall into time, into tune, with the ground beneath her, with the night, in her newest garden. She stood there, a sapling, willing herself to take root.

CHAPTER TWO

Lily started on the clearing, beginning with the nettles, set her pattern quick; striking in tough with the best spade she'd found, lingering some on each down-strike, leading with her right, forwarding steady as a soldier, delicate as a dancer.

Strong then, Dan thought, passing unseen, he assumed (wrongly), on the woodland side. Stronger than the arms suggested. Something stony in there, too, entombed.

'I'm not sure about her,' he told Harry in the room that Harry (in keeping with the two generations before him) called The Morning Room.

'You're not sure about anyone,' Harry said. His gaze shifted to the window, picturing Lily working, flowing; mind on her task.

'There's something about her – held back,' Dan said. He had more coffee in his mug, from the pot in the kitchen that Irene made, clockwork, first thing. He sipped it. He was a full-lipped man with eyes that were dark enough to lend a little drama to his brooding.

'You didn't like Tish either,' Harry said.

Dan hitched one of his brooding eyebrows.

Harry laughed, good-humored from company and sunshine. But then less so, suddenly, pinched by the recollection of the finally-summoned plumber, tinkering now in a second floor bathroom, tools spread about on the black and white tiles – forty-five quid an hour, plus call-out. He sighed and there was sadness in it. 'She's good-looking and she's willing. And my energy for...all this, is limited. I need someone to put a bit of wind in my sails.'

Dan didn't answer, but strayed his eyes to the window, too, hearing again (though only in imagination) the orderly thup...thup...of the digging.

At the door, Irene, holding the second cup of coffee she allowed herself, 11:00 a.m. daily, listened and felt the rip of the attack through the remnants of her feelings. *Someone to put a bit of wind in my sails* – Irene liked to think that she did just that. Irene liked to think that she was more than the cat's mother.

Later, when Harry went searching for Irene, wanting the checkbook, he couldn't find her. Typical, he thought. No one about when you want them. No one to rely on.

Irene knocked on the flaked blue of the garden door before entering – treat as you'd like to be treated. That was Irene's heart's philosophy. She had brought coffee for Lily.

Lily leaned her spade against the wall and approached her, taking off her gloves as she walked. They were not gardening gloves, but the sorts of gloves that Irene's mother might have worn, years before, going to town on the bus. Irene admired them.

'I sometimes wonder who wore them before me,' Lily said. 'What adventures they've had.'

Irene did not mention her mother. 'The color reminds me of the way the ocean always looks in travel brochures,' she said.

'You could wear it,' Lily said. 'True blue, Forget-me-not blue, the color of faithfulness. It goes with your complexion.'

A Friend, thought Irene, kind, but too beautiful to understand what crumbs these were – what you could wear, how you could fix your hair – to a plain woman.

Lily, catching the moment's hesitation, switched the talk to the magnolia; asked if Irene had noticed when the first buds had appeared.

Irene hadn't. 'But there are journals somewhere, garden notes – in the library, I think.' Lily could ask Harry.

Lily nodded, but she was staring out now, not hearing the greenfinch chatter, or seeing the dappled wood light, not listening, just remembering. 'Look,' the woman had said. She was an old woman, or had seemed old to Lily, then, and gentle. 'There's a picture of a lily in it. A lily, like you. Isn't it beautiful...Like you?' How many people had spoken to Lily that way then? Not nearly enough. 'You can keep it,' the woman had said. It was a book with three hundred pages, cumbersome for a little girl, but Lily had kept it and taken it with her – town to town. The book had had not one, but dozens of lilies in it. *Lilium: Enchantment, Davidii, Henryii, Connecticut King.* And, best of all, *Lily-of–the-Valley.* She had traced the letters with her fingers, mouthing the names, and marveled at the photographs. Then she had found them, come to life; out bus windows, along the footpaths of her childhood, in other peoples' window boxes, other peoples' gardens – she had stood and stared. And had her head slapped for daydreaming.

'Do you have you a plan?' Irene asked, watching her. 'For the garden.'

'Of sorts,' Lily said, turning back to her, to now. 'But with spaces in it for Happenings.'

'I could be your apprentice perhaps,' Irene said. The two of them pals. The two of them with things to do. Forget about running after Hopeless Harry indoors. He'd be sorry, she thought, not forgetting him at all.

'Maybe you could,' Lily said. The wattage of her smile overwhelmed the evasion in her answer. She liked to choose her successors with care.

Irene stood, took the half-full, cold coffee cup from Lily's side and shook out the slops.

'Save me the grindings,' Lily said. 'Slugs won't crawl over them.'

'You're not one for coffee, though,' said Irene.

'Not so much,' Lily said, though she'd thanked Irene effusively when it was offered. 'Not lately.'

'Noted.' Irene made an entry on the perpetual list in her head to pick up something more suited and went back to the house feeling useful, her heartbreak – now so much frivolousness – in wisps.

Midday, and here came Ruth; nice woman and cleaner, temporarily turned sea serpent by the hose of the vacuum cleaner; which was coiled around her neck. She had her arms around the obstinate body of it, but the cord was dragging and the plug was clinking along behind. She'd been to Mr Mender in the town. Mr Mender had a door sign that said: Keys Cutting. And a window full of clocks, and re-soled shoes, and flies, and last summer's dust. The shoes were rubber-banded in pairs and put into a paper bag when you collected them.

Ruth had paid twenty-two pounds and forty-five pence to collect the Hoover (new parts and a work-over) and got a receipt – handwritten, from one those books with the numbered pages and carbon between. The receipt was folded exactly in half, corner to corner, in the zippered pocket of her blue jacket which was hitched up now, at the side, by the infernal bother of the lugging. She'd give the receipt to Irene. Irene always saw her right. They were battling the same odds, Ruth and Irene, except that Irene had her heart in it and couldn't turn off from Motthoe at night, when she was watching the telly, like Ruth could. Not that Ruth didn't have her hands full, with two teenage girls to chivvy and a husband who spent less and less time helping, or caring, or coming home.

Ruth pulled the cable, and drooped it over her arm. It was all she could do to lift her feet today – no matter that they were shod for marathon running. Her girls, Jess and Ashley, fifteen and thirteen and a half – tall as her if they bothered to stand up straight – had stopped out 'At a Friend's'. Then Rob, rolling himself back late from an evening of watching his sorrows reflected in the base of a pint glass, had decided to play Dad at 11:45 p.m., pacing and threatening. It had been drained faces all round this morning. No-one had eaten properly and the girls had been late off to school. Again. Rob – a day's work on a building site, a mate to pick him up, car idling and tooting at the gate – had left without a goodbye.

The hoover trundled over the flagstones. Ruth with her stomach straining at her t-shirt and her buttocks escaping her jeans, heavy with life and lardy with hardships.

'Good afternoon, Ruth.'

There was Irene in the kitchen, lit up as the High Street at Christmas. Maybe his Lordship had given her a bit of encouragement. In her heart, Ruth hoped not. It wasn't that she had no time for Irene. She had, more than. And precisely because she did, she didn't want to see her wading in any further, into the mire that was Motthoe. Ruth did not want to see Irene sinking down with Motthoe, and Harry the Dreamer's big old sack of half-baked notions. You'd like to see Irene get a break, have some fun. Living with her Mum like that – a carer, at home and at work. You'd like some light stuff for Irene.

Ruth put the vacuum down, a hunter laying out a carcass. 'All right?' she said.

'All right,' Irene told her. 'There's coffee in the pot.'

Ruth poured the coffee – the last of it – and lifted the top of the machine to remove the filter and dead grounds.

'Oh,' Irene says, 'keep those.'

Ruth stopped, cold coffee drooling through the paper over the sink, eyeing Irene.

'Slugs won't crawl over them,' Irene said. And the smile flared yet more.

After that she told Ruth about Lily. Gardens Loved, she explained.

One More Dreamer, thought Ruth, her chest filling and deflating with the head-shaking. One more without the sense God gave them.

'You can dig a man right out,' Lily said.

Irene – exerted and panting lightly, with her crew-neck discarded – reddened. 'None I'd want to,' she said, eyes sliding to Lily.

Lily, eyes sliding to Irene, said, 'Works on other troubles, too.'

'Good,' Irene confesses.

'Dig,' Lily tells her. 'Dig like you're drilling for joy.'

And they dug. Side by side at it. Making more than the time of two, once they were in a rhythm. Irene's Troubles loosened with the clod.

By three o'clock Harry had joined them, fitting himself between the pair in the action, taking Lily's orders with lamb-like docility. Hup-to with the spade, hup-to. They dug mostly in steady silence, three sets of thoughts in the air above them, sun coming down warmer than you'd expect, so early in spring. Harry ventured this observation lightly to Irene, but she dismissed it.

'March is often hot,' she said, giving him no latitude.

Lily, watching them, assessed them as a pair. No, she thought, daffodil and onion, best not mixed.

Ruth, done in the house (main living quarters on alternate days – dust and a doing – four of the bathrooms spritzed) came down and propped herself against a wall for a bit, watching too, and thinking more or less the same thoughts as Lily. But Ruth wasn't a Propper by temperament and soon took up a trowel. Four of them now. The sounds of the work cheerful. The sun was dipping, but the warmth was in it still. Ruth said she'd known the beginning of March to be like this before. And some lovely early Easters, when Jess and Ashley were babies. At the beach, she was thinking; Rob grinning with a kid on his shoulders and a canvas hat on his happy head.

Harry was outnumbered and knew it. He accepted his status with the impassive resignation of a rural vicar.

They were all individually content in their industriousness and kept it up until Ruth went to the house to fetch drinks and a St Clement's cake, she'd made the night before – knowing that no one in her own family would eat it. The sugar on the top of the cake caught the light like the water in the bay when she set the tray down on a garden table, with a one-leg-wobble, that she'd pulled around from under a tree on the other side of the wall. The table had been used last by The Gigglers, and a friend of theirs who'd brought a ouija board, to an out-of-hand Friday night gathering at the Nanny Flat just after New Year. Their shrilling – set off by the surprise tottering of the table's uneven leg – had woken the woods at 2:00 a.m.

'Hi then,' Ruth called. 'Fuel for your exertions.' Five o'clock.

Lily washed her hands under the garden tap. Harry held back behind her and ushered Irene's turn next with a gentlemanly sweep of his arm. It was the brightest afternoon Motthoe had seen for quite some time.

Ruth and Lily and Irene sat on some slatted chairs and Harry perched on the wall behind. Ruth took a second slice of cake and ate it without tasting it, almost without chewing it. Wednesday; her girls were supposed to be at netball practice. She'd lay money that they weren't, but she didn't want to think about it, so she convinced herself that they were. She reached out and picked up a lump of citrusy sugar with her fingers. Sweet, sweet, of late her best comfort. She repositioned herself on her chair and sighed.

'Elderflower,' Lily said of the cordial that Ruth had brought with the tea and cake. It was in a jug, topped with sliced lemons. 'Do you make it, Ruth?' she asked.

'My mother makes it,' Irene said. The fading of her voice and the smile that moved only the bottom half of her face told a much longer tale than the words did.

Ruth, Lily noted, was watching Irene, like she cared. Ruth: companionable as lovage.

'I take home the blossoms for her from the tree on the path near the old hedge maze.'

'You do most of the work, I expect…' Ruth says.

Now some real amusement – sneaking upwards across Irene's face. 'All of the work. But if you asked mother, she'd tell a different story.' Tittering here. 'When the sugar is heating, I'm to stand over it – waiting for her to shout at me to take it off the element. It's surprising the volume she has in that titchy frame.'

She was laughing for real now, giving everyone else leave to laugh, too, at the forlorn funny of it – the adult daughter hunched over the saucepan, the birdy mother squawking, the grim, annual, unchanging ritual of their cordial making.

A car sound cut in on them, crackling from the gravel beyond the wall.

'Dan,' said Harry. He stood and went to wave Dan in to join them – he was that filled to the brim with *joie de vivre.*

Dan, framed by the door in the wall, surveyed the work. Anyone who'd known who his father was – a rock star, living more than comfortably from royalties and the ministrations of his fourth wife, a man who'd found peace with Buddha and two sets of children since Dan was born – would have seen the resemblance.

'What do you think to our efforts then, Danny boy?' Ruth said.

'Not a lot of point to it is there?' Dan said, but in a voice not too harsh, since it was Ruth who'd done the asking. Motherly Ruth, who answered some need in him.

Ruth, deflated, became aware again of the nip of her waistband at her mid-section and didn't answer.

Irene, muted too by Dan's pessimism, slumped.

It was up to Harry to jostle them all, to keep the thing

from tipping and rolling down again into the ditch-water that had been the Motthoe mood for some time now.

'Of course, there's a point,' he said. 'Isn't there, Lily?'

Lily, silent, but not unnerved, smiled – always a reward, but directed at Harry a benediction.

Look at the fool melting, Irene noted, like ice on a gas ring. She heard the hiss in her head and thought of Mother at home with her village woman carer, waiting for Irene to get back. She thought of the soup they would have for supper – slopping on the bedclothes, a washcloth in a bowl for bathing the papery skin. Who'd do that for her, she thought, when her time came?

Lily stood and faced the T of the brick pathway and began to speak. Not loudly, not seeking attention, or audience – nevertheless they were drawn in.

'Lavender edging,' she said, 'here…along the path, so that the scent catches you on walking. Agapanthus all to attention at the back…Alliums.' Her arm unfolding like a swan's wing. 'Webs of cosmos and echinacea, and coreopsis and wallflowers there, and larkspur in front. Dianthus, nepeta, nemesia, zinnias.' Index finger striking each chiming note like a stick on a xylophone. 'And there, roses, and there… beyond, fringing and welcoming the woods, primroses, aquilegia – granny bonnets…' It was a poem, mesmeric. She had traveled the length of the pathway on those fine feet of hers with her skirt tucked up at one side – just enough to make Harry hurt. 'And,' she said, spinning back to them so that the skirt unhitched itself and fell to her ankles again – a curtain at half-time, 'all in amongst, love-in-a-mist.' She stopped, recitation ended, serenity emitting from the immaculate face.

Everyone felt the calm of her. Even Dan. Irene wanted to applaud and almost did. Harry grinned – recognizing a fellow star-gazer, but one with the skill to lay it out and to follow through. Not like him, Harry the Dreamer – he knew his reputation. He knew that all his wishes escaped him like unhitched balloons.

'I like marigolds,' Ruth said. 'But the slugs beat me last year. Came down one morning to the stalks. Horrible stunted stalks where the flowers had been...all that yellow and cheery gone dead and ugly overnight. Nothing left, but horrible stalks.'

Lily advised Ruth to save her eggshells and...

'Coffee grounds,' Ruth finished – an 'Aha' lighting her face.

'That's it,' Lily said.

Dan, still leaning, not quite caught in Lily's images, coughed. He'd seen Ruth's eldest in town (school hours) with a lad – a scruff and a layabout. They'd been smoking, the twosome, on the wall by the mini-mart, the girl's pleated skirt grazing her thigh tops, a discarded ale can at her feet. Ruth was going to need more than marigolds to cheer her when the trouble from that came calling.

Ruth got up with the unnoticed grunt that had delivered from her regularly these last twelve months (bending to pick up Rob's newspaper, climbing the stairs to look for the girls) and clattered the tea things together. Dan took the tray from her and she smiled at the shyness in him before passing. She'd be off, once she'd washed up. See you tomorrow.

Irene got up, too and looked at Harry. He was sat on the ground now, arms resting around his knees, looking at the garden with Lily's pictures in his head and her bewitching extremities in touching distance. Irene lifted a teaspoon that Ruth had missed and waggled it, as if clarifying the need for her own departure – off then…

'See you tomorrow,' Lily said, turning.

Irene took the spoon, caressed the tiny hallmark with her thumb, and left.

Lily, sorry for Irene's aching, which bled from her crimson, put her turquoise gloves back on and tugged at their wrists.

'Back to work?' says Harry.

She answers with her spade. Lifts it high and wide, then…thunk.

What a woman, thinks Harry. *What a miraculous woman.* He gets up and lifts his spade high and wide. Thunk.

Ruth's jeans were undone at the waist. They held, though, because they were stretched so tight over her hips and thighs. It was a struggle to get in and out of her car – a beaten-up, metallic-blue thing as spacious as a thimble. Small people, the Japanese, Ruth thought, creaking her way into the gap behind the steering wheel that was often narrowed further by the need to pull forward for Jess's long legs to fit in behind. Jess's knockout long legs. Both Ruth's girls had inherited their father's build… lanky, that whole family. Ruth was glad. Glad they got something useful from him. Sports Day when they were nine, eleven, they'd run like gazelles the pair of them. First in all the races, clearing the hurdles with blue-sky ease. Jess could take a stile in two moves. Knockout long legs. You didn't care for yourself, didn't care how you looked, when you had daughters. You cared about them.

Ruth removed her jacket – should have done it before she got in, her arms stuck with the need to wiggle forward and no room to do it in. Eventually she got it off, breath coming gusty. She was wheezy now at the smallest effort. From above, the rolling bulk of her mid-section was not a happy sight. One more in a list of unhappy sights. She dragged the t-shirt down, pulled at it, to cover her underneath. She would have to do something. Eventually she would have to do something. But now, she reached for the quickest comfort. Chips for tea, she thought. The girls would be pleased. That was what mattered, that the girls were pleased.

Irene, though she knows the foolishness of it, having delivered the spoon (rinsed it and propped it in the drainer) and collected her things (padded jacket too warm for the day and a black leather handbag from Willett's, bought six years ago, now giving at the stitching) hesitates at the garden door, propped open still. It frames Lily and Harry – almost silhouettes in the lowering light, six paces between, but joined nevertheless in motion. A pair, she thinks, but sun and moon.

She walks to her car, parked at the stables and follows the route Ruth has taken a few moments before, out past the front aspect of Motthoe, past the lawns once emerald and tended, past the pathway to the ornamental lake – no longer ornamental and sadly lacking in Lake – and she heads down the hill with the view of the sea, and down to the gates and out, signaling left, onto the main road to Falston, only ever busy at holiday time – not very busy even then.

As Irene nears the home she shares with her mother, as the traffic thickens and the houses become even-spaced and boxy, Irene's spirits flatten with the landscape. She parks in the driveway of their vanilla bungalow with the reverse alchemy completed – a heart turned to lead – gets out of her car and walks the concrete path to the frosted glass-paneled front door with a condemned man's tread. The grass is growing, soon it will need cutting, she thinks. One more job for Irene. She cuts the grass herself with a hand mower – one ear cocked for mother's bell.

'Hello,' she says to the neighbor woman who sits with Mother in the afternoons. She drops her worn Willett's bag in the vestibule beneath the photographs of her dead father on the wall.

'She's been asking for you,' says the neighbor woman, nudging an eyebrow down the short hallway. The neighbor woman, who is a churchgoer, but more relevantly, a saint, makes no complaints about Irene's tardiness (twenty minutes). She puts on her jacket and smiles – wishing her luck. It takes all Irene's Motthoe pay to keep the neighbor woman coming, but it is worth it, to get out. It is worth every penny for those winter days when it's just her and Harry, fire-lit.

Mother's voice, tin-can edged, spikes its way down the short hallway from the end bedroom. They have three: one for her, one for Mother, one for clutter – an empty suitcase in the wardrobe, from a long-forgotten holiday, and a china Pierrot on the window ledge, staring out, fixedly smiling at the cul-de-sac between the net curtains.

'Irene? Is it you?'

Who else, Mother, thinks Irene? Who else?

Forty-eight minutes later Ruth pulled into her own driveway; end of terrace. First house and only house that her marriage had bought – room for a loft, never realized. They'd moved in after Ashley was born – the second baby, and last, though Ruth had longed for more. Rob was still working at Drew's then – foreman, before the layoffs. Bedroom for Ruth and Rob at the back, girls at the front – a room each. Now the curtains are drawn in Jess's room. They are always drawn; the child is allergic to light.

Ruth has stopped at the convenience store – double-parked, what the heck, and bought burger patties to go with the oven chips. Buns and iceberg, film-sealed tomatoes. It's still warm, maybe they'll put the ketchup on the outdoor table and eat there off birthday-leftover paper plates. Everyone will laugh. And help clear away. When was the last time?

It is silent in Ruth's house.

Then not. The Layabout Boy, bold as you like, is on the landing. No shirt on him. Chest brassy and black jeans slipped over his shimmy hips.

'Oh shit,' says the Layabout.

'You're right,' says Ruth.

At Motthoe, late, Lily puts her spade down.

Harry, hungry, massaging one shoulder with a soil-streaked hand, wants to ask her in for a whisky, but she is matronly brisk in her tidying up and offers no opening. Ah well, thinks Harry, he can wait. He congratulates himself on this victory of restraint and says he's going up...lingering nevertheless, while expecting nought, which is what he gets.

'Night then,' she says.

In the deepening dark, Lily drinks from the standpipe, leaning to it. The water rush is pleasant across her lips and chin. Then she takes the tools into the greenhouse, which is up to working standard – only two panes missing. She has cleared one bench already and sets to on another, wiping down with suds in a bucket she's had from Ruth. Zinc buckets piled in the old laundry – she'll talk to Harry about selling some, knowing well enough he'll do anything for her – wanting to go careful, though, in case she puts him wrong.

Inside the house, Harry looks at the chimney in the yellow sitting room. The inlay is flaking off. With morose dedication he begins to flick more of it into the cold grate. There is magnificence, sometimes, in absolute ruin, and mild dilapidation has its charm, but a vast middle ground exists between these, exuding only wretchedness.

Harry stood there some while, and then he lifted his lonely tumbler of whisky and set off morbid on a Rot Tour. (A title he had invented, and often said out loud to himself in the grip of masochistic dispiritedness.) Harry was particularly prone to set off on a Rot Tour when he had been drinking whisky. People said that gin was a depressive, but Harry, who associated gin with tonic and tennis and totty, even if all those things had been sparse in his life in recent times, found whisky to be the true dimmer – as if the Scots had added Dour with the water so that its effects were at once inebriating and sobering. Harry thought it perfectly possible that he was the only person in the world thus afflicted. There were so many things about Harry's life that seemed to him unique. Anyway, there he was, whisky in hand, setting off on a Rot Tour, like a kid picking a scab.

A lot of the time Harry did his best to forget about the house. He lived mostly in two of its rooms, between visits to the kitchen, but, from time to time, he braced himself and did the rounds, as if this alone were testament to his preparedness to do his duty by Motthoe. As if by inspecting his legacy, familiarizing himself with its difficulties, reminding himself it was there, he wasn't shirking. Harry also thought, but this may have been the whisky, that if he just had one more look – this look, this night – some answer might come to him, some inspiration might dawn, or flash – some single, all-improving, all-encompassing way forward. Harry wanted so much to find a way forward, because if he didn't, the Rot was going to include him soon enough. Maybe it already did.

He always began at the central staircase and – one foot solid on the tatty runner, big toe to the first stair rod, right hand light on the mahogany banister – breathed in a great courageous breath of grit and determination there, as if the ascent ahead of him was vertical. Rising, he took in the half a dozen pictures on the wall on his left-hand side. They were all framed similarly, in gilding that had turned bronze, they were all in need of cleaning. There were two he liked. He had never much thought about why, although, if pressed (he never had been) he could have articulated his preference for a painterly approach. At the first floor, he dog-legged left and opened each door he came to in turn. There were a series of large bedrooms (six) to this side and three bathrooms – two full, one a tacked-on shower room modernized in the 1980s. The bedrooms were, on the surface, pretty enough (the yellow and the fern green particularly charming). They had views, and beds with carved bedheads, and ottomans, and mantles, and mirrors – oval and cheval. They had wallpaper. Two had attached dressing rooms. They kept most of their flaws to themselves until some hurried bit of lifting, or shifting was undertaken in pursuit of a sock, or a mouse.

The last room was full of junk. It was junk that Harry remembered: two mattresses (stacked on their sides), an abandoned kettle, a tea trolley and a tray (still with medicine bottles on it – used for his father in his final illness). There were two, truly ugly oils – landscapes, in black frames (one with broken glass) and a pair of large urns (one cracked, one missing a handle) – majolica. There was an electric blanket the color of gums, folded, with a frayed lead and no plug, on top of some copies of *Shooting Digest*, and a tower of curling paperback thrillers. There was a bookcase that listed. There were several lamps, most with crooked, stained shades. Harry stared at these things and felt inertia flood his limbs and overrun any good intentions. The junk just... was. Always had been. He shut the door on it and began back along the corridor and down the passage on the far side to his father's room.

Harry opened the door to his father's room and went in. Not redolent of damp, this one, but of his father. Harry hit his whisky, a little hard, and looked around; his father's bed, a wing chair, a large mahogany blanket box – two plaid blankets folded neatly on top. An empty bud vase, a travel alarm clock on the bedside cabinet. He had been in this room more often since his father's death – four unremarkable occasions – than he had during the man's lifetime. It was a room that meant nothing to him.

Once Harry had finished on the first floor, he went on up to the second, then the third – front line to the roof. Here the rot, as in the dark areas at the rear of the ground floor, was even more evident. There were buckets at intervals along the corridors. Harry slalomed evenly around them – he had learned to negotiate them in the poorest of states. He opened door after door; store rooms, small, mean back rooms – once servants' sleeping quarters – and took in, through the thickening whisky haze, the fallen plaster, the broken door hinges, the rust-marked bath tubs. Then he descended, by the back staircase and came out behind the pantry at the rear of the kitchen. These rooms he glanced at, but did not spend time in. He wound through the passage out into the front entranceway again and turned right and went into the library and the billiard room and the music room in turn. Each dim, each dejected, each like a once-fine woman, grown drunk and debased and suicidal.

Lily, moths for company, puttering still, is aware that she likes Harry – in the way she might be aware of a strand of hair on her cheek. Lily liked most of her garden owners well enough. As a rule, they weren't gardening folk, just folk with gardens. When she was younger, Lily had been perplexed by this strange chasm, on one side of which were people with resources enough to put land around them, but not to care for it, people with balconies full of under-watered begonias and sodden busy-lizzies. People with no plant sense at all – nattily dressed women, men with the look of golf about them. They could walk past dying leaves and not hear the cries. But she had understood that this was how it was, and that she could profit from it. Make a life.

'Well, yes, it could do with…' they'd say, gazing fog-eyed past her at their gardens as if trying to recall how they'd got them. But then they would look back at Lily with concern in their eyes; for their family's safety, for the small change they kept in their kitchens, for their portable electrical items.

Lily would tell them carefully, picking her way across the swinging bridge to their acceptance, about other houses she had worked at, watching their worry withdraw a little and seeing their eyes roam back to the scraggy pansies.

'I just don't have the time,' they would say, as if she had berated them for their neglect.

Lily would tell them that time was more precious than pearls. And they would relax some more.

'What could you do?' Their eyes now sparkling with visions of Versailles (on the cheap). That was when Lily would lay down her back-pack and walk them through. Talk possibilities.

The newer gardens had usually been poorly planted. When she worked on those, she found neighbors tended to catch her eye over the boundaries and ask: when she was finished at Kate and Tom's, could she pop over. But she liked best the big, aged houses, rambling at the village edges, the houses whose gardens had been loved once, but got out of the hands of the present owners, or the elderly ones – teary to see their irises again – or the young couples who were delighted with her plan for the disused carp pond, who sent their children out to help her with their bright boots and bell-shaped coats on. Don't go Lily, the children would say, when she did. Their mums, especially the lonely ones, the ones who'd moved to the country without thinking about the hours they'd spend without their husbands now that the commuting time had doubled. The lonely ones loved Lily, wanted her to move in: gardener, au pair, companion…But Lily cleared the weeds, filled the ponds, planted up and left. She showed the mums and the kids how to look after things once she was gone, showed them how to hang colored sheets between the trees to make play-rooms, told them when to harvest the damsons, employed nice local lads to help out the old ladies. Lily the Tiller, Gardens Loved.

In all these years of selecting, in all these years of scouring locations and choosing the one that was just right for her purposes, Lily had only really cared for one or two, though she had left some tenderness in all of them. Lily saw her work as creating gardens for others, not for herself – matching the garden with the owner. That was her task. But now, here at Motthoe, which she had chosen for its perfectly isolated aspect, here, she had walked through a wooden door in a red brick wall and felt her knees weaken the way knees do when arrested by love. It had been, that first day, a moment of absolute knowing, that this garden was The Garden. The One.

Lily worked now in the gentle haze of her aroused affection, quiet, efficient, till just after eleven when, behind, came the smell. Lizard fright infused her even before the voice hit, mountainous.

'What have we here, then?'

Ogden; Motthoe's tenant farmer, year-round tanned, and shoulders for calf-wrestling – fetching half a lamb up to the kitchen door. He's supped one, or four before he's come, though he's not a true drinker. Widowhood – in Ogden's case an especially desolate landscape – sends him in search of companionship with his supper and it is most reliably found at the Dog and Duck.

Lily, spinning, knows by the tilt of him, the state she's dealing with. Not young, on the crest of grizzled, but strong. Not truly drunk. Sober enough to be dangerous, if he is. She hasn't decided yet. She whips a broom into service, stiff across her chest, and positions herself military steely.

Ogden is not, as it happens, an aggressive man, merely cantankerous and never a danger to women. He sees the fright of surprise turn granite in the girly's eyes and holds up his two hands – declaring no evil is obscured there.

Lily, broom still to attention, eyes no softer, waits.

Ogden now straightened, less for the drink because of the effect he sees he's having on her, lowers his hands again, minimizing himself. But the conviction from her emits nevertheless.

'Don't mind me,' he says, backing off from the dead-fish flat of that eye, shuffling now – no roaring to him – he's just unkempt, and a bit hapless without a tractor to guide, or a wife at his side. He slips off, up the pathway.

Lily remains armed, the splintery press of the broom handle stiff against her palms. A lime hawk-moth makes a low, solo circle above her head. Outside all is black and still. The blood resumes its course in her veins, but nothing else of her moves. She is stone.

'So,' says Dan, watching, soft in the silent dark, Labrador's muzzle in his hand, one knee in the grass, 'there's the kernel.'

Chapter Three

The weather has continued temperate since Lily's arrival at Motthoe. Harry's television set is tuned permanently to the Twenty-Four-Hour News channels (earthquakes, uprisings, floods, famines, politics and fears for stock prices) which is, he finds, an excellent way to escape the demands of the immediate, and the half-hourly weather reports are lately augmented with loving footage of English girls gone sun-worshipper in the parks; stretched on the crisping grass in their lunch hours, dark glasses obscuring their upturned faces.

'It's more like July,' says Harry. It is the thirtieth of March.

Babies and old folks all over Britain are sucking cornets beneath lurking seagulls.

Dan scoffs. They are in the smallest, ground floor sitting room – a wide white hearth and a Knole settee. Of Motthoe's rooms it is one of the most pleasant and liveable. There is a portrait of Harry's mother over the fireplace – dressed in a gown of eau de nil, beige blonde hair and blue eyes like Harry's. Younger then than Harry is now, the years left to her could have been counted on one of her ringed hands, but that particular pain is burning constant in nobody's breast any more. Teeth no longer gnash on that account. The loss is accepted and its effects, though felt, are no longer specifically attributed. She hangs there, Harry's mother, monumental and fading.

'It's twenty-one degrees,' Dan says. 'Why do people in this country make such a thing about weather?'

Dan does not think that it is hot. Dan has been to Ghana. In fact, Dan is widely traveled, having left his job in advertising and his girlfriend (also in advertising) in his mid-twenties, to see the world and to get his father's attention. He has managed both, but less dramatically than fancied. Then, back from years of comfortless airports and fate-dictated sleeping arrangements, visiting Harry – whom he'd known in the past only vaguely, through mutual school friends – Dan had found a willing, undemanding listener. He had told Harry some of his traveler's tales and hinted at his plans to write them up – his illuminations in fictional form.

Harry, looking for company, had suggested Dan stop on, in the apartment above the garage. And Dan had done just that. On and on, with his Olivetti. But Dan has fallen victim to the crash of impotence – his thoughts are not so zingy in actual form. They have died on paper. The sparse words like corpses. The vim of Dan's stories has receded inside him, leaving only a dragging sort of shame for his ambitions. His self-esteem is as supine as his prose.

Dan's coffee-drinking arm moved up and down now, and up and down again with morose, unvarying motion.

'It's not hot,' he said, sternly, full of glums. His own fails and lacks were even darker lately in the light of the hard work of the girl, Lily – week on week, day on day, hour on hour, creating something substantial out there from rubble and desert.

In her garden Lily is washing her clothes under the standpipe, ready for hanging in the morning when the sun first hits the east facing window of Ashcott's kitchen – she could wash her clothes there, in Ashcott's ample basins and sinks, but she doesn't. She rotates her skirts these unlikely warm days – one worn, one washed – and spreads them, inside-out, on the holly, to dry. Or drapes them over a bit of tomato twine to flap for a while . But she needn't because Ogden has fixed her a washing line. The first of his Provings.

Ogden's cottage was not unlike Lily's, (which, like all locals, Ogden only ever referred to as the back valley cottage) except that his was entered by the kitchen door. There was a front door, but Ogden never used it and no one that Ogden wanted to speak to ever came to it. The back door had a porch, added by Ogden in 1987. He and Mary had been married for six years, then; anniversary of wood. The porch was about three-foot square, covered with corrugated roofing. There were two steps up to it. Ogden had laid the concrete himself – boxed it in, borrowed a mixer.

The porch had a shelf running along its two flat walls at a height of four foot – that had been Mary's suggestion. It was a narrow shelf, just wide enough to rest a bottle of milk on, or a set of car keys. In the summer Mary had put house plants there – African violets and streptococcus – with coffee container lids for draining saucers. Ogden has never removed the pots, they linger there, their long-dead cargo turned to dust, ring-marks on the paintwork beneath them. A small, neat pile of logs, cut to eight-inch lengths, lived in one corner, next to a steeple of newspapers – web-joined by a long-gone spider to a feed sack full of lightings, fished from the river's edge and left to dry so long that now they sparked almost upon sight of a match. There was a coal bucket, half full, and a second metal container with a lid, brimming with ash.

On the night that Ogden left the half lamb at the big house kitchen, and frightened the girl in the greenhouse, he came to his porch of dead things, turned his key in the latch deftly, and entered his kitchen just as smooth as if he had not spent any of the evening at all in the Dog and Duck. The kitchen smelled of wood smoke, though the stove was cold. The wood smoke smell was permanent and filled the entire house – the walls were yellowed by it and the ceilings were bronzed near the fireplaces.

The kitchen was small. There was a drop-leaf table under the window – both leaves lowered, Formica topped, pressed to the wall. There were two chairs, Mary's high and firm with a cushion at the back and solid arms for her stiff getting ups and slow easing downs, and Ogden's, softened by wear and permanently shaped as him. Off the kitchen, on the opposite side, a door led to a pantry and a scullery; rows of empty preserving jars above the freezer. It was the kind of freezer a body might turn up in – a big rectangle with a hinged top. Mary had not used it toward the end for fear of toppling in. Somewhere in its depths languished several bags of gooseberries – harvested on the late June day when they had first taken delivery of the thing, plugged it in and watched it, waiting for the bells and whistles. The lamb's other half was in there now, too.

There was a hall in the cottage that led to the rear side of the stairwell, and a small lobby where the unused front door let in some light by the stained arch over it. There was a telephone that never rang. To the left a dining room, last used for purpose at Mary's funeral. Now it served as an office of sorts: paperwork pertaining to the farm – yields, rotations – spread about. The sitting room, on the right, was darkened by the net curtains at its window and the heavy ruffle across the top. It was a bay window with a window seat – Ogden had never moved Mary's needlework bag from it, and there were cushions with washed-out chintz covers – blue and yellow. Ogden never saw these things any more than he might see his own, sun-spotted skin. A clock on the mantel that ticked… an old people's clock, its dreary rhythm ticking away the last years of Ogden's life.

The stairwell in the hall led up to two bedrooms, one a box room, full of the belongings a static life of seventy-odd years gathers – mementos and things that need mending. In the corner was Ogden's bedroom, taken up almost entirely by the bed, with its velour covered headboard, and a wardrobe – Mary's wedding outfit still inside, packed in camphor and sandalwood.

Ogden had removed his boots, that night of the half-lamb and scared girly, in the kitchen and hung his coat on the hook by the door, set and lit the stove and taken from the shelf above it a can of rice pudding, selected carefully from fifteen identical cans, before he had gone upstairs. Upstairs, he took three pounds in loose change from his pockets and left it on the table at his side of the bed and turned the lamp on before he went back downstairs to sit in the kitchen while he waited for the stove to heat sufficiently to render his rice pudding lukewarm, which was the way he liked it. He began to read yesterday's newspaper, but he did not take to it much because into his mind kept coming the beautiful face of the lass with the eyes terrified as a rabbit's in a trap.

Three days after their greenhouse encounter, Ogden went back up to the house to see Lily in daylight to stop her haunting him. He chose 11:00 a.m. – a blameless hour and Irene nearby, fetching clippings from the rose bed in industrial overalls.

'Hello,' he said, soft as possible, coming up to Lily's front side so as not to spring. He kept back, aware (as he was not, generally) that he smelled of cow muck.

Lily stopped in her work – two garden forks and one foot to the root clump of a daylily – and looked at him. No fear, but wariness there still, Ogden thought.

'Startled you some…Tuesday past,' he said.

Lily waited.

'I'm sorry for that,' he said. 'I can be bawdy when I've had a few.'

Lily had seen men twist from warlock to wimp before, but she saw none of either in Ogden now. 'No matter,' she said simply.

But then she smiled, and Ogden smiled back, before she hit in hard at the daylily clump and split it clean.

A Doer, thought Ogden, repay her in kind. And so, he had fixed her a washing line out back of the cottage because he had seen her skirt on the bush, with the holly pricks tenting the cloth.

Lily, while she had yet to use the washing line, had marked the effort and engraved a plus in Ogden's credit. Since then, he had begun to build a compost frame – to her specifications – and enlisted Dan and Harry for the conveying of an ancient cattle trough to the garden – to be planted with white petunias. She had taken to making a list in her notebook: *Ogden?: Attach trellis. Replace greenhouse panes?* (He had swiftly solved this last with glass from a second smaller greenhouse, now abandoned, near the empty lake.)

Today he had brought her up some thick gloves – once Mary's for the gooseberry harvest, but he did not say so. Although, maybe the meaning in the gesture was somehow passed to Lily because she put her hands together, as if to pray, before easing the fingers and knuckles of the gloves that had grown stiff with winters of unwearing and thanked him particularly warmly. She intended to take on the *Gertrude*

Jekyll that clothed the pergola. It did not look at all spectacular now, but Lily could see it already as it would be in late May, could imagine sitting underneath it on the painted bench that would be there by then and inhaling the ambrosia of its scent. Mary's gloves would be just the right thickness.

The *Gertrude Jekyll* was, to Lily, the queen of the garden – the other flowers so many pretty handmaidens. She had already planted garlic at the bases of all the roses and hung fat balls for the birds to ease their insect problems, but a queen demanded a different level of attention. After Ogden's departure Lily approached this one as gently as she would have a shy horse. With one boot on the low wall at the border edge she lifted the other lightly up behind until she was standing close enough to see the points on the glamorous old girl's thorns, and said, 'I will be gentle as moonbeam, if you don't fight me. But I expect you will.'

Slowly, surveying the woody unproductive stems, the suckers, the beginnings of buds, Lily lifted her secateurs – battered handles, but tips sharp enough to rival Gertrude's own. She stepped in and began, moving about the bush with deft calm and watchmaker precision. The old rose whimpered as her taller reaches were plucked down and snapped her gangly ends at Lily's face, but a wide red beret, worn low as a pruning hat protected her from the worst.

'Play nice,' Lily said, and laughed – silver bells amongst the bloodless clippings.

By the time she had finished, and straightened her hat from the angle it had been forced into by a snagging runner, the plant looked, incredibly, vivified.

Dan had watched Lily all the while in this operation.

He had never known the rose in bloom and had no idea of its variety, nor heavenly aroma, but now, because he had seen the thing offered such a dose of applied tenderness, he felt tender toward it himself. *Is that the story of all things?* he wondered. *Does love and care beget love and care?* Yes.

Dan watched longer, as Lily fetched a fork to load the wheelbarrow with her cuttings, took off her hat and loosened her hair. She looked back at the rose and smiled. 'Good morning ma'am,' was what she said, but Dan was too far away to hear her.

And what of Ruth, these weeks past? More had been uncovered than the bold of the Layabout's chest, which had been seen off quick enough.

'No mettle to him,' Ruth had said to Jess. 'Couldn't give two pins for you, foolish girl. Throwing yourself away.'

Jess, deaf to it, shrunk in a chair, knees drawn up, ring-eyed as a panda, chewing on a finger, said nothing. Misery and sulfur resentment leaked from her.

Then Rob, on time for once, had come home and the whole sorry story had been retold. What had Ruth hoped for – solidarity? None came. More yelling. Nasty names. The little sister, Ashley, banished upstairs to her own business, earwigging and crying on the landing. Doors banging all over. All gone bad.

Much, much later, in the dark of her bedroom Ruth, listening to the roll of her husband's breathing, thought: Nothing. Nothing to draw her there. No pull from that sound anymore, nor the scent of him, nor the radiated warmth of his skin, pocketed under the duvet. Not the way there had been once, the pull was gone. The comfort was gone.

Ruth got up, took a toweling dressing gown from a hook on the back of the bedroom door and put it on. Rob slept. Erratic hours this last year and a half had turned their lives into one of those diagrams with the overlapping circles, except that the overlap had shrunk and shrunk, like an old pea. They neither of them stirred anymore when one left the bed – once the forging bow of their family ship.

On the landing Ruth opened a cupboard and reached up to the top shelf, patted behind with her flat hand, behind the hat she'd worn to her cousin's wedding, behind the nice green table cloth she kept for best – pressed and folded – patted behind them, feeling for the box with the baby things in it.

Downstairs Ruth sat at the table in the dining room they never used and took Jess's first shoes from the tissue that had gone thin and soft. She held them, in all their white weightlessness, one in each hand. She closed her eyes and felt the baby's foot through them – cool, the way baby's feet always are. She could see the teeny toes. 'Long,' it was one of the things people said: 'Look at the fingers, look at the toes – they're so long.' And the fingernails – precious replicas of something else, shells. Moons. Everything there. She had stroked those tiny hands, those tiny feet and marveled, the way a mother must, at the flawless engineering, the perfection that was her own child. She had felt their infant cries inside her, the yank in her chest.

Ruth could still feel her children's cries. She could still feel the contraction beneath her ribs at that sound. They're still crying, she thought, it's just coming out different – all muffled. She put the sweetheart shoes back in their box and closed the lid, firm with decision. She would keep Jess near her. Not just near, next to her. She would glue the child to her. She would take her to school, she would collect her from school. She would spend every minute with her. Quality time – that was what they told you. Maybe it wasn't too late.

When she told Rob, he rolled his eyes. Couldn't be doing with it, he said. One bust-up after another. The girls were turning into brats (he blamed her, Ruth heard that). But Ruth stood to it anyway and told Irene she would come up earlier, leave for an hour to collect the girls and come back up to Motthoe with them – leave later. Irene doesn't mind, nobody minds – as long as Ruth comes.

Now she sits, every day, engine idling at the school gate and watches the mass of pleated skirts and supermarket trousers. She watches them scrabble out in singles and gangs, guessing the bullies, guessing the bullied; the smelly, underworld life of high school. If the girls don't dawdle, she makes it back to Motthoe by 4:15. Longer evenings now, she does the same work – gives the girls the option of a hoover or a hoe after homework – they always choose the hoe. They like to be out with Lily. No matter to Ruth – they look nice with a bit of sun on their faces. How long will this weather last, the papers say another week.

It is because of Ruth's girls, Jess specifically, that Lily has her second true encounter with The Gigglers. The spicy pair of renters who Irene had told her about. The ones living in the old Nanny Flat. They had first met when The Gigglers, linked like bracelets, had come back, pink with liquor and dateless, on a Thursday night, around 11:00, with their work jackets over their arms and fitted tops under, showing off their bosoms. Cute and round as Labrador puppies all over, those girls, and about as steady. Arm in arm, they were supporting each other on heels that were no good in gravel. They'd taxied back. Lily had heard the thoop of the doors and looked up from inspecting the clematis that surrounded the exterior of the garden door by torchlight, to say hello.

'Ooh,' they spun together, the second one nearly on her rear. 'Hello.'

'Hello,' said Lily. The half of the automatic outdoor light that was still operational was tripped by their lurch in her direction and flooded the driveway. One girl shaded her eyes.

'You're new,' she says.

'A new one,' says the other. Funny this, they laugh. Their heads lolled inwards.

'One of Harry's is it?' says the one.

'A new one,' says the other.

More laughter.

Lily smiles at them. 'Gardener,' she says.

'Oooh,' they laugh and laugh and laugh, shoulders meeting, gone goose-bumpy now, tottering round to the mud room door, and the two bedrooms, bathroom, sitting room and kitchen beyond (the Nanny Flat, long since vacated by Nanny). They have painted all the rooms themselves with bargain priced rollers and a couple of quarts of pink emulsion from the home improvements store.

Since then, Lily has seen them hurrying to work mornings sometimes, sharing the one car.

''llo' they call out, flapping past, dangling keys, pulling their hair back. They both work in the Building Society, one on the information counter: Yes, madam, how can I help? Lived all their lives in Falston, went to school together, played netball together, went package holidaying together when they were seventeen. Known to every boy in a twelve-mile radius.

The next time Lily talked to them properly things were different. Things always are.

Ruth's girls – defiant, indulged, but their good mother's children at heart – bucked at the new supervision rules, but submitted to them though they were moany with it. Moany, moany, moany... it washed over Ruth. Too many other things had worn her down. If she couldn't save her marriage, if her looks were gone, if her lottery numbers never came up, she could still rescue those girls from the likes of her own future and she intended to do it. And, any case, her heart went out sighing when that boy didn't call. She saw Jess checking her phone, checking and checking. Her heart went out, despite herself. That low-life maggot never even called. It was this that cemented Ruth intractable; she would set her girls up for better. Oh yes, she would.

At Motthoe in the afternoons she put her daughters to work. Lily, assessing each, suggested light weeding for the younger one, watering for the older, and smiled assurance at Ruth when she came out to check on them. Ruth was silently pleased, standing at the raised end of the plot with her arms folded. Buddha Foreman.

Then, one evening, as they were packing to leave, Lily said, 'If the afternoons haven't worn you out, you might like to help me at market on Saturday.' Lily was a believer in the restorative and unifying powers of meaningful work.

'What's it worth?' Jess said, risking some lip, hip jutted into a saucy S, thinking to earn herself, at least, a fiver for a trip to the High Street – lip shine in a pot, mascara, gubbins for her hair.

'Never you mind about money,' Ruth told her. 'Effort bears its own rewards.' She was telling herself. Re-telling herself things she'd forgotten, fighting for her life and theirs. She had been reminded, through the magic already wrought by Lily's industry, of the possibility of Overcoming. She stared that child of hers down, she could have lifted a car right then and everybody saw it.

Reluctance is an armor more easily pierced when worn over youth. Jess's was dissolved by the fatty whiff of the sausage rolls that Ruth bought everybody from the vendor at the open arch of the market entrance. They drank tea out of flasks and stood, stamping their feet on the cobbles that had hosted cattle and cheese sellers and bakers and candle makers in their time. Little birds hopped the beams across the high draughty arches above them. It was perishing cold at setting out time, 7:00 am.

Lily had been to market several times already – taken different things depending on the day. Saturdays: tied bunches, flowering plants, terracotta pots, old gardening equipment, and, experimentally, some painted-up garden chairs (Ogden). On Thursdays – day for the real gardeners, more the farmers, or folk who fancied themselves so, knew their geraniums from their pelargoniums, knew what citrus they preferred in their marmalade – Lily potted up cuttings from Motthoe's rarer plants. On Thursdays she bartered time and expertise, once hired herself out for a morning and put the cash back into Motthoe. Harry, who knew nothing of the costs associated with gardening did not notice, but Irene did and her friendship with Lily, fed by these small generosities which were so in line with her own, blossomed.

Lily liked the market. Liked going home with the cash and counting it up with Irene, liked deciding how to spend it, liked bargaining with other sellers for trays of annuals and seeds for her patch. A new hosepipe. Two new water butts. Much had already come this way. Cash in, cash out. Lily had lived like this her whole life and understood it. Lily's mother, in the good times (few) had been quite the trader. She had never sold her own stock, but got herself work selling for others by offering a morning's free labor – plus a bonus if she sold her quota. She always did. Always took home her thirty quid in folding.

'You don't want to take government money,' Lily's mother had said. 'Pay your own way and the bastards don't own you.'

Town to town, market to market, lost all the brass on the bingo, in the boozer. Lily sitting at the back, running around the field, or the village hall, or the main road – wherever her mother had left her. People gave her left-overs, broken toys. Lily had begun to hang around the plant stalls as soon as she was old enough, and when her mother was not up to working, she'd brought back her own money. That was how they'd met him – he'd been hocking plastic dolls (off the back of a lorry) and passed one to Lily, 'Too big for one of these now, I suppose.' He'd laughed and Lily's mother had laughed. He was of the same philosophy as Lily's mother: Don't let them own you. Don't let them find you. Pay your own way, although soon enough he'd let Lily and her Ma pay his.

Lily wondered why the market memories didn't suffocate her the way other memories did. Maybe she had always found enough light-heartedness there, among the noise and the smell of food, the protection of strangers, to comfort her, to block out the rest.

Harry joined them that morning, along with Ruth and the girls, for the first time. He'd abandoned his bed, his walk, his reveries for commerciality and currency, for graft – the lure of Lily.

'What do they want them for?' he said. Lily had sold some wooden handled hedge clippers to a husband and wife – trim, dressed for the second home.

Lily laughed. 'They'll look appealing, leaning against their patio wall,' she said.

Harry shook his head. He liked talking to the people, liked the people around. Liked people.

They made a record four hundred and ten in readies with the last of the daffs, pottings and cuttings and some antiquated scuttles dandied up with plants (drainage holes drilled in the bottom, with expert neatness by Ogden). Jess had hit the swing of things and proved herself a tidy little trader: 'Some daffs with that for the Missus, sir?' Afterwards, they all celebrated with cordial and cider back at Motthoe.

Ruth, Lily, Jess, Ashley in Lily's garden, drenched in Good Feeling. Dan there too, though up aways, alone on the lawn. Ogden not far off from that with Harry, discussing a crumbling stone border wall, when who should come walking, sauntering by – shirt on this time, but looking as usual half dressed – with one of The Gigglers (Em) tucked under his draped arm and his coasting right palm, but Jess's errant Layabout.

They don't see him at first, but hear Em's titter and then his low provocation and another squawk from her.

Jess, glass at her mouth, quits listening to her sister and stiffens. Her eyes turn animal. She puts the glass down very slowly, but gets up fast. The slatted chair topples and Ruth, who has recognized the voice now, too, says, 'Jess, he's not worth it…' But to no good because Jess has already shot out through the garden wall and run and leaped and sprung.

Em, the Giggler, squawks for real now. Jess has grabbed Em's hair and manhandled her off the fella, who she's managed to backhand larrup – the element of surprise being on her side. Jess is screaming at him and calling him all the things Ruth has called him in her head. But now comes Em from the rear, tugging at Jess's own hair and calling her things, too, so the boy ducks out and lets the women fight each other. He's legging it, but Jess sees him and flies herself after and Em after her.

It is Dan who halts progress, stands squared on in the Layabout's path. The Layabout can't divert because there's a crowd closing in. Dan is only his equal in height and weight, older, probably an easy enough mark, but there's a black Lab taking note at his feet and behind him is Ogden. Harry and Lily are back, flanking Em – not a bad lass, but put-out and riled shaky.

Ruth and Ashley have Jess.

'You'll be leaving now,' Dan says, menacing quiet. 'And you won't be coming back.'

The boy, curling his head toward the girls – chests heaving, commotion still crackly in the air around them – hitches his lip ugly at one side and says something to Dan.

Dan looks at the Layabout for a split beat before shoving him hard, both hands to the chest, pinning him to the garage wall, and jamming a no-messing fist to the little goon's jawline. They breathe each other's breaths there for several unreeling seconds, then Dan steps back, though his expression still means business. Loosed, the boy sizes up his situation and stalks away, fouling the air behind him with abuse. Driving off in a black, made-over saloon, he takes the first corner badly.

Giggler number two, Kara, has joined the unhappy party and is hearing from Em-the-wounded about Jess's mad cow antics. Jess, sunk to the ground, is crying, and resistant to comfort.

Harry, edgy in the estrogen, joins Dan and Ogden. Dan gives his fist hand a shake and Ogden says: 'I would have, if you hadn't.' And Harry looks at Dan, bemused. You think you know a person.

Now, Kara, on her friend's behalf, trots smart to Jess with her backside bouncing like beach balls in a bag and her hands on her hips. But she has to melt her defiant stance to duck down to Jess, and then, when Jess raises her tear stains and looks like the kid she is, some of Kara's self-righteous fury drains.

'What were you thinking?' she demands, but not as harsh as she started out.

'You're all better off,' Ruth says and reaches a hand to Jess, who takes it at last and stands up.

Nobody knows what to do then. The gas has gone out of the situation, but Normal isn't resumed.

Lily raises one of her bud-birthing hands, beckoning, or blessing. She has picked cow parsley and cranes bill and oxeye daisies on her dawn walk from Ashcott this morning; laying them across her elbow-crook like a mother rocking a sleeping baby. The rough little bunch is in water now, on the shadowed side of the greenhouse with no home to go to. 'Would you like some flowers for your kitchen windowsill?' she asks Em and Kara.

And Em and Kara, slightly blind-sided, unable to fish up an objection between them, say, Sure, Yes, and follow Lily like the kids in Hamelin. And then, so does everyone else.

It is the first time The Gigglers have crossed the blue door threshold.

'Ooo,' says Em, snaking her hair back behind her ears and adjusting her straps. 'It's gorgeous.'

'Gorgeous,' says Kara.

Jess is still crying, but silently (all the more plucking for the heart-strings around her). In the sanctuary of Lily's garden, Ruth extends both her arms and this time her daughter doesn't fight her at all – Love, the only salvation.

She feels her other, younger child – historically the compliant one, but living in her own head most of the time now – she feels Ashley's hand reach and rest on her shoulder. It is warm through her blouse. While Jess, the clever kid, the rebel, shakes and sobs beneath her chest, no resistance left.

'I didn't know he was spoken for,' says Em, softly. 'Just a bit of fun.' She is holding the flowers that Lily has fetched for her, leaning her face to them, looking at them as if they were something new and exotic, though she drives past wild banks of the same daily.

Jess doesn't raise her head, so Ruth speaks for her.

'Nobody's fault, love…' she says. 'And he got what was coming.'

'See his face when Dan whomped him,' says Kara.

'Shock, or what?' says Em, grinning.

'What'd he say?' chimes in Ashley. 'What'd he say to make Dan so angry?'

'Never you mind,' says Ruth. 'He got what was coming.'

The Gigglers have got doughnuts in their kitchen. Brought them back last night from the late-night supermarket, along with the Layabout. They go in and fetch them, put the flowers on their windowsill as suggested, come back and put the doughnuts – peace cakes – on the garden table in their supermarket packaging. Ruth puts more coffee on and Lily fetches arnica ointment for Dan's hand.

'Not even Easter and it's hot enough for July,' says Em. She unhitches her shoulders from their shoestrings, cake in hand.

'Sweltering,' says Kara, toppling dumpling beside her.

Dan takes the ointment, surprised still by his own reaction to the Layabout Boy's vileness; the spring of defense in himself and the use of a fist.

'Thank you,' says Ruth. 'Standing up for her like that.'

Ashley – thirteen when she remembers, eleven when she forgets – hugs Dan: chaste and spindly armed – Our Hero. And Jess, drawn back from her spacey gaze into the nothing of the middle distance, focuses, and fixes her almost-sixteen-year-old attention on him – the way a duckling does on the first thing it spots after hatching.

At dusk that evening Harry and Dan, more securely bonded than they realized by their motley-bachelor winter together – canned stew and matching corduroys in the weak heat of the Aga – walked with no prior discussion to the neglected, no-longer-lake – silt and bulrushes, clogged stream channels, self-seeded trees some twenty-foot high. In its centre a small island (the creation of which had been overseen by Harry's great uncle, with hoarse and hands-on instruction) housed a folly – a circle of Doric columns beneath a wing-topped dome. It was Harry who struck out for it first, disturbing the sideways cling of a fluffed sedge warbler, but Dan did not need any urging to follow. Mud and foul algae slowed their progress and clung glutinous to their shins, slime slithered over their boot tops and filled their socks and crept up their thighs, but they were laughing before they reached the little crumbling shrine – as pointless as Lily's wildflower gathering and just as picturesque. Harry was first up onto the dry of the structure and he reached a hand to Dan. They stood, looking back over their tracks in silence, side-by-side, till Harry stepped up again and in, under the dome. It was just wide enough for him.

'Feels like I'm standing in my own tomb,' he said.

Dan looked back at him. 'You look noble, actually. Like the emperor of something.'

'I'm not emperor material,' Harry said. He stepped out again, onto the narrow strip of earth that sloped into the swamp below them.

'Do you think it matters?' Dan said.

Harry sat on the folly edge and brushed his hands together, thinking. 'I think leading is over-rated, but blind following is worse.'

'What's the alternative?' Dan said.

Harry looked at him, wondering at this: this conversation, a depth in it that weeks alone together had not plumbed, had not even dug for. Dan; he barely knew him really. They had become housemates by default, linked by loneliness. Now a friendship was apparently germinating. He thought about Dan's question. 'Fellowship,' he said and stood and struck an emphatic foot back into the bog.

On Sunday morning, Ruth dragged Jess, exhausted and frowzy, from her teen-dark purple pit .

'We're all going to sit down together today,' she says to the resisting eye-lids. 'We're all going to sit down together for a proper family Sunday lunch and we're all going to bloody well enjoy it.'

Rob, always tempted by beef – Ruth has chosen it

purposefully, a supermarket special – says he's off for a pint before lunch, back at 12:30. And Ruth says, 'Fine.' She makes Jess peel: parsnips, potatoes, swede and carrots. She tells Ashley to get out the decent china that was their gran's. She gives them a few stories about their gran and doesn't care if they listen. She pats salt over the beef the way she used to, the way her mother used to. She's bought apple pie for pudding – gets Ashley to whip the cream after she's topped and tailed the beans. Tells Jess to put some music on. They're going to bloody well enjoy it.

They laid the table together and later, when the meat smell starts to fill the house, there's happy in it. There's family in it. They're all going to sit down together. Ruth goes upstairs and changes her clothes. Puts on a dress that doesn't quite do up at the back. She bought it for a long-ago holiday – more than five years and ten gained pounds since.

'You look nice, Mum,' says Ashley.

Ruth looks at Jess. The critical daughter-eye coming sideways.

'You just need a bit of lipstick,' says Jess. It is a thank-you. A thank-you for not ranting on about that business with the Layabout, a thank-you for seeing the hurt still in her, a thank-you for being Mum. She goes upstairs and fetches down some of her own lipstick, but Ruth doesn't think it suits her.

'The dress won't do up at the back,' she says, and they all have a bit of a laugh about that.

Jess tucks the open sides under. 'You've got nice skin, Mum. It's all right to show a bit, you know.'

One o'clock.

At Motthoe Lily rakes and rakes the sun-soaked soil of a new narrow border to a fine tilth.

At 1:30, Ruth drains the fat from the beef dish, stirs gravy powder into the leavings, adds water from the kettle.

Lily makes drill holes with a cane for the sowing of night-scented stock, dribbles the seeds from between expert thumb and forefinger, covers them lightly.

Two o'clock. There is a fly in the window of Ruth's dining room, buzzing behind the curtain. Ashley shoos it out with a paper towel.

Lily pokes hazel stakes into the bed to support the abundant growth to come.

'Call him,' Jess says to her mother. 'Call the pub.'

But Ruth doesn't. She goes into the kitchen instead and begins to dish up, slices the beef with her elbows out. Slices it into nice thin strips and forks it onto the plates. Then she shares out potatoes with a big, slatted spoon. Jess and Ashley put the rest of the veg in the serving dishes and take them to the table and Ruth follows. They all sit down and ignore the one place empty. They dish up. The shoulder of Ruth's dress keeps slipping down. She jerks it back up a couple of times and then stops bothering.

It is Jess who stands and serves the fourth plate: beef, potatoes and Yorkshires, cabbage and carrots, cauliflower cheese.

Jess with the plate; at waist height, not rushing, not dawdling – calm, like an experienced server in a five-star establishment. Carried it out of the dining room, through the kitchen and across the linoleum in the tacked-on room that Ruth had once called The Conservatory – only once, the kids had laughed and called it that all the time afterwards, pulling their faces so that their noses elongated. 'Oh, I'll just put it in the Conseeeeeerrrrvatory, shall I?' 'Ooh yes, please. Next to the polo pony.' Ha ha.

Jess walked round the back, by the path that skirted the house, the gravy glossing in the outside air, through the gate and past the car. Down the length of the street, then past Mr Corden – hedge trimming. Past Katie Bevan – in her seventh month with her third – filling the paddling pool with a hose for her other two, bouncing next to her in their bright nylon swimsuits.

Ruth and Ashley following Jess now, coming out by the front door. They saw her clear the corner and turn left on Allan Drive. Ruth noted the way she held herself – dignified, in her cute shorts and flat shoes, her hair hanging, bobbing at the back in a Sunday pony-tail. Ashley ran after her.

'Come on, Mum.'

Ruth came, left the door open.

Jess crossed the street and walked two more blocks. The plate at the same height. Then she crossed the street again and walked through the beer garden and into the back bar of the White Hart, where the light was dim and the boozer smells came from the carpets and the walls and the breath of the patrons, where the publican wiped the wet circles from the bar with a damp teacloth and knew people's names. Knew Jess's Dad's name. And there he was. At a table with Tom Widden and Ian Squires – Tom a bachelor: odd jobs. Ian a manager at Drew and Sons, with a family of his own at home. It was Ian saw Jess first, nudged Rob.

Ruth arrived – her lungs heaving and her nostrils flaring at the effort of breaking into a sprint on the last stretch – just as Jess leaned across Ian to set the plate in front of Rob.

At first nobody spoke. The bar was silent. The street was silent. The world was silent. Birds settled in the trees, silent. A chap at the bar twisted with a smirk that signaled a smart remark, but none was forthcoming. He pocketed his change and lifted his pint and watched hard over it.

Then, 'It's your dinner, Dad,' Jess says. Voice cool.

Rob – Dad – says nothing. Perplexed. Embarrassed. Angry. Face fighting to settle on one.

'Mum's made it. It's lovely,' says Jess. And she turns to leave. Her dear little bottom in their faces, blue-denimed and high on her schoolgirl legs.

'Come on, Mum,' she says to Ruth.

They walked home, three abreast, arms linked, feeling the hot pavement through their summer soles. Katie Bevan's kids, in the pool by then, slapping the water into crystal spray with their star-fished hands. Squeals carrying like gull cries across the dried-out grass and up, and up.

At Motthoe: Lily, mindful, eyes rising to the clear sky, set out two, thin, hole-ragged bedspreads ready for use as covering in case of frost.

CHAPTER FOUR

The only time she'd traveled back to see her mother, Lily had been forced by logistics and a sticking clutch to take a bus. The bus smelled of classrooms and raincoats, but it had stopped right outside the hospital where her mother was dying. It's a miracle, her mother had said, that brought you to me. It was, Lily supposed. Or at least a strange sort of chance.

Lily's mother had settled somewhat, those last years. (Too late for me, Lily had thought. Too late to do me any good.) A proper roof over her head in a decent enough block, petty vandalism out front; a cast of doing-their-best single mums and old people and lads with their hoods up, a couple of sets of young-marrieds playing hard at nest building – TVs on tick. Lily's Mum complained about the kids, the noise of them in the halls, blamed them for the uprooting of the plants by the walkways.

It was dogs, Lily said, that scratched at the flower beds, ill-trained dogs and squirrels. Kids weren't doing it.

Lily's Mum had lost her phone, or had it nicked, or flogged it, who knew? Anyway, Lily had called her via a neighbor's landline, maybe twice in three years, and not talked long. Then, one night, two years before she'd come to Motthoe, Lily had phoned again – December, month of lichen and leaf mold, forced hyacinths and foil-wrapped poinsettia – from a call box on the road, between gardens. And the neighbor had said that her mother was in hospital – lung cancer – going fast. Lily ought to come. And she had. Because there was something she wanted to know.

Lily's Mum, dying for sure, and no more forthcoming than she ever had been when she was not, turned away when Lily asked her. Had she not even suspected? She had coughed so rabidly that Lily had thought she would never get her reply, that any response would go with her to wherever she was going. Then: 'Can't you leave it alone, Lil? It's so long ago. It's all forgotten.'

Forgotten, thought Lily, saying nothing.

'The man is bound to be dead and soon I will be, too. We didn't lead the kinds of lives that last. He's dead, I'm sure he's dead.'

Why was she sure? Lily urged. It seemed urgent.

'I just…Nobody's heard from him in years,' Lily's mother said.

And Lily had known then, grown clammy sick with the knowing, that her mother had tried to find him. Had wanted to find him. Lily had known that her mother had wanted the man to come back to her. She didn't speak again and neither did Lily. She waited as her mother turned her head to the spartan hospital wall and, after coughing again lightly twice, seemed to be drawn into it, lost. Four hours later she died, leaving Lily on a journey without terminus.

Harry's ambles have begun to crystalize into Walks. They have embraced Destination. Today: out, deliberate, through the other side of the woods, across the field and down the dip to the cliff path. A light wind ruffs his hair and presses his shirt flat at the front. He carries his father's stick; malacca, ivory knob-topped. His elbow is bent and his forearm tipped upward to accommodate it. From a distance he looks just like his father walking those same cliffs, but there's no living thing about to observe this, except an osprey who is dedicatedly cruising for fish. Harry stops and watches the osprey carry its catch away, its hooked talons having barely disturbed the water surface in plucking it out. Planning, thinks Harry. Planning and experience; the underpinnings of successful execution. He plants the stick between his astride legs and considers.

Then, on the way back, where the path widens and a pine branch curves across it so that you'd have to swerve hard if you were on a bicycle, there is a dove sitting on a branch that would be just high enough to scooch under if you were a small boy, and so inclined. The dove sees Harry from her swivel eye, but waits until he is almost at her before she flaps and beats off through the clear where the clouds scud cotton to the horizon.

Such mornings these, Harry thinks. Harry has begun to notice them, and other things besides. It is as if he has been sleeping, and is just now roused.

'*Had I the heavens*,' he recites to himself, '*embroidered cloths, Enwrought with golden and silver light...*' Harry fairly rattles with these baubles; well-polished fragments from a casually attended education and an elemental attraction to all things lyrical.

He takes the route that will bring him to Lily's garden – he thinks of it thus, 'Lily's Garden', as do all others who are familiar with it. Almost there. He comes to a precious posy of wood anemone and is able to name it. He remembers his father tapping with this same stick at the white flowers and raising his eyebrows at him, at a very small Harry, four, maybe five.

'Wood Anemone,' said small Harry – diction neatly clipped, little chin well up.

The stick was flourished. 'Good,' said his father. Then, a little further along, the stick rapped again.

'Anemone!' announces small Harry. Shouts it almost, thrilled at the possibility of two Goods, two awards from his father. But his father had sighed – not anemone, sorrel.

What would it be like, thinks Harry now, to father someone? To have a child's teaching in your hands. Could you raise one on dreams?

Lily is not visible in the garden, although she will be about, Harry knows by now – industrious and hidden, a sprite. He stops and looks around from the center of the brick pathway, sunlight washing over her handiwork. It is as if she has brought these bright days with her – so endowed with them they've been since her arrival. And now her garden, like an infant's smile, is drawing things to it. Drawing things to it and emphasizing (the way all improvements do) the defects of its surroundings.

Harry walks back up to the house, with something new in him, something almost vigorous, to wait for Irene.

Once Harry is gone Lily shakes the past from her head, smooths the kinks from the hosepipe and stretches it out. She feels groggy from strange dreaming, she has been napping in the greenhouse, a new habit – swift sleepings, twenty minutes, or thereabouts, on a pile of husk-smelling burlap. She turns the tap and walks the length of the pipe and lifts it as the water burps and flows. She pins a finger over the nozzle to spray her wildflower seeds – she has given the new back bed that edges the woods over to them. Ogden has built a fence there of hazel hurdles, to screen this section from the main garden until the box that Lily hopes to combine with the yew for this offshoot of the hedge is established. Maybe a bird-feeder, too, a seat in the wall – a spot for thinking-on,

Ogden has suggested. Lily has not objected.

The warmth of the early spring is setting off the insect life, but it is not a yet a drought – there have been showers in and out, mostly at night, garlanding the nursery webs and their cargos of spiderlings with rain pearls, bringing the earthworms to the surface, sending paunchy snails on ponderous journeys along the stonework. The moisture has helped with the gladdening of things. Spring is working its wizardry.

Lily walks the beds with a fingertip to the hose nozzle, makes the water into a glistening sheet while the clouds still give good enough cover, before the bright rises too sharp and magnifies the droplets on the young leaves. Then she's back to her greenhouse for more early work before Irene arrives and needs an ear.

Irene is fed up with her tatty black Willett's bag and its sticking zip, but there it is. She has had a bad night with mother, who has called and called for her – plaintiveness and irritation alternating – at 1:00 a.m., at 3:00 a.m. Irene hefts the bag off her shoulder – Atlas unloading – and drops it onto the thick pine table top in Motthoe's kitchen that has done sterling work there for near a hundred years. She undoes the bag and fossicks for the Motthoe checkbook which she has taken home with thoughts to balancing it. She hasn't.

'Had a few thoughts,' Harry says behind her.

Made her start.

'Thoughts?'

'Ideas. I'd like your input.'

Irene does not find the notions of 'Harry' and 'Idea' incompatible, but his demeanor has lost the nebulousness that usually accompanies his presentation of them. Generally, when Harry has an idea, he rushes at you with it, breathless from a four-minute reading of an article by someone in Sweden. Or, late, with a drink in his hand, he tips his head to one side and shares a few lightweight suggestions – dawdling them out in disconnected billows, to no audience in particular.

'Coffee?' he asks.

Irene, one hand still buried in the cavern of her handbag, felt her jaw jar downwards. But Harry didn't see it because he was fetching out the cups and the milk and the teaspoons, just as if he had made her coffee every weekday morning for the past eleven months. Instead of Never, which was the actual statistic.

Then: coffee made, both cups having been carried up by Harry, there they are; Harry and Irene, opposite each other at Father's desk in The Study. Not in The Office with its dusty box files and chock-filled ring binders and forest of lost receipts. Not in The Office, where ballpoint pens go to die with Irene's spirits – but in The Study. Irene had never sat there with Harry's father, whom she had always called Sir. Although she had, once or twice towards the thin end of his life, taken notes at his bedside – he blanket-covered from the mid-chest down, button pajama'd above. Motthoe, as now, decaying softly around them.

Irene had only worked for Harry's father for six months (prior to that she had cared full-time for her mother and done a little book-keeping piecemeal), and had taken her instructions from him mostly in the form of notes, composed in the late evenings and conveyed to her desk for her morning perusal – single-spaced and copper-plated. Irene's lot had never been a plum one.

Today, saffron light is pouring through the upper half of the sash window of a lofty room that is part of the original 1704 building. There is an early twentieth-century, eight-inch globe on the mantle, and a needlework fire-screen on a stand beneath a large, foxed, but handsomely framed print of an archer (weapon primed, two eager lurchers held back by a kneeling servant at his side). The Persian rug is the exuberant, flowing color of claret.

Harry, on his side of the leather-bound blotter, is talking sober. And Irene, on hers, is listening, forgetting about everything, even her bad night. Even Mother.

'Sunny spots,' Harry said. 'That's where I've gone wrong.'

'I see,' says Irene. She jots down 'sunny spots' on a ring bound reporter's pad – maybe it'll come clearer in the writing. It doesn't. She looks at him, expectant.

Harry smiles. Irene feels it in her solar plexus.

'There's enough here that is working – can be made to work. We need to develop it, start small and build on what we've got.'

'Yes,' Irene said.

'Like Lily does.'

Irene felt this in her solar plexus too, this name in his voice, so caringly expressed. A small snort escaped her. It really had been a rough night with Mother.

'No,' says Harry, misinterpreting. 'Hear me out.'

She will, of course.

'Up till now I've been looking at big pictures...too big. Missed the wood for the trees, if you see.'

She saw.

He squared his shoulders. 'What's the income from the rent... from the two girls?' he said.

She told him.

'What do we do with that?' he asked.

'Pay me,' says Irene.

A still moment. Three hundred years' worth of dust motes in the air between them.

'Well,' says Harry. 'That's good.'

'And Ruth,' says Irene. Thinking to make it better. Not sure what.

'Good,' says Harry again.

Irene is stunned. How is it that he has never thought about this before? Two young women alive under his roof – how has he never thought about the finances? Lord Harry of Dreams.

'We need more things like that – regular payers.'

'Yes,' says Irene, thinking the B&B notion is to be resurrected. Not much better really than his other unhinged suggestions: music festivals, windfarms, fourteen acres of Fijian fruits...

'But we've got to work like Lily,' he says sounding almost solid than ever – cautious, but confident, too. 'Take one patch at a time,' he says.

Irene does not want to spoil the morning, but this is the time to tell him: The Gigglers have found somewhere to live in town, conveniently located for Jezebel's. They had told Irene this, two days earlier, by telephone, as if Jezebel's might mean something to her. As if she might care. She didn't , but she knew what Jezebel's was – you don't miss much if you live in a town the size of Falston (one three-screen cinema, four coffee shops, a library, two florists, three restaurants, half a dozen chain-stores and Willett's – two floors, family-owned for ever). Jezebel's was a sort of nightclub. There'd been a Grand Opening. Irene knew this because she'd seen the posters. Anyway, in addition to the central renovation of the building – previously a saleroom for tatty bric-a-brac called Antiques Barn – two flats had been built in a strange side building. The flats had been hard to let, on account of the inbuilt noise factor and high likelihood that someone would sleep, or worse, on your stairwell most Friday or Saturday nights, and the rents had been lowered accordingly. The Gigglers had not been able to resist.

'We're giving a week's notice, because we pay by the week,' Em had said.

Irene could remember many occasions on which The Gigglers had not paid by the week, and one particular weekend when she'd driven up specially and knocked on the door first thing, to chase up a whole month's worth. The door had not been opened. The sound of muffled giggling behind it had transported Irene back to school. Loathsome school and the loathsome sense that someone was always behind a door giggling, that you were getting it wrong, that you were wrong – the constants of Irene's life. She had walked away from that door pulling at the front bit of her hair – horribly wayward that morning with early rising and unseasonal humidity.

Harry, *re* Irene's finally delivered news, The Gigglers are leaving, was concerned. He hadn't kept track of the rents, but he liked The Gigglers about the place. People. Ordinary people, with jobs. Harry liked those sorts of people about the place. They kept it from feeling dead. The problem with most of Harry's schemes, and he was aware of this, was that they attracted, not so much life, as people who were escaping from it. People who upped and left when the music did, when the sunshine did, when the food and the bonfires ran down. The Gigglers were going, too, and another part of Motthoe would be empty. Empty rooms rot fast. He said this to Irene.

'Yes,' Irene said. 'They do.'

These small agreements didn't mean anything to Harry, but they meant something to her. The ties that bind. She thought he was looking a bit glum again, when she left him. He had lost some of the puff of his new stuffing. She wanted to put her hands on his shoulders and say: It will be all right, we can do it. Though of course that would have been silly on every count. Silly Irene. She to be giggled at.

Dan had come upstairs, looking for Harry. Quietly. Dan had the rueful man's skill for skulking. Harry had been in The Study with Irene. Dan heard them talking in there, but not what was said – the rim lock of the six-paneled door was sealed. There was a tone though, a carrying tone, in the timbre of Harry's voice that breached this barrier. Dan was glad to hear it, but mildly sorry too – even Harry would revive, and run, and leave him behind.

Dan left off looking for Harry. He had had no particular

purpose in doing so in the first place. It was just that a person who has little to do, and ample time to do it, is better distracted from this fact by another person in the same situation, than he is by his own company. Dan made his way back down the lightless rear stairwell, stairwell of the unseen, of servants and workers, out through a side door, tradesman's entrance, on Motthoe's south-western corner. He crossed the field and noted the flattening of the grass where Lily crossed twice a day from Ashcott, but struck out diagonally across it to a field where Ogden had put two calves. He wondered on the fate of the calves, leaning against the fence when he reached it. One of them came towards him, dripping saliva and leaves from its rubbery mouth. Dan met the creature's eyes, but did not reach out to it, or call it, cooing-voiced, like a tourist. Or a fool.

As he watched the creature Dan wondered that so large an animal could still look so young. Dan did not remember ever feeling young himself; not in that way that implies innocence. He thought he had probably never looked young (he had). He remembered, always, feeling old. Older than his peers, older than Harry, although Harry was his senior by eight, or so years. He had been a shy boy – the lot of many sons with no particular talent and fathers renowned for one. And he had worn, unintentionally, a permanent expression of withdrawal that others often took for surliness, until, in the end, that was what he had become, crusty. In the course of the past winter, Harry had started to become that way, too. People are catchy. Harry had said things about himself that were downing. His face had begun to give off an air of unapproachability. He had been turning into Dan. Dan, who wore his personal gloom as snugly as an old scarf, had been shocked to see it on someone else. Especially someone as open-hearted and decent as Harry. Harry, who never questioned Dan's desire to write, or lack of desire to write, or anything else. Harry, who had let Dan live at Motthoe all year and had asked nothing of him other than his company.

Dan leans on the fence, runs his eyes along the horizon that is tinged lime with sunshine, listens to the wet breath of the calf and realizes that he is happier at Motthoe than he has ever been anywhere.

Ruth had made her unhappy decision at 12:45 p.m. the night before, but not then had the means to implement it. An hour and forty-five minutes after closing time. Ten minutes after Rob slammed the bathroom door on her hand. It had been an accident, but he'd been too drunk to notice what had happened. Ruth had sat in her kitchen, in the dark, with a packet of frozen corn wrapped in a tea towel, thanking God that the injured fingers were on her left side – she would still be able to drive and wield a duster cloth satisfactorily.

Rob was in bed by then. She could hear him snoring. It was possible, because this was more and more frequent, that he was not actually in the bed, but on it. Some nights lately he slept in his clothes – took himself to the bathroom, pissed like a horse, careened into the bedroom and fell unconscious there, rather than asleep. She knew that he did not know that he had hurt her hand. Once she'd have taken him to task for a transgression like this straight away, but now, even physical pain left her biting her lip. What was the point of another row? What was the point of waking the girls? Jess: so like her dad. Didn't they always say that when she was little? Jess in her vest and romper pants, diddy ears sticking out of her wee bald head – so like her dad. Now, they'd be screaming, they'd be at each other's throats the pair of them, in minutes. Ashley would be crying, with her hands over her ears.

No, better to sit there in the dark with her fingers throbbing, the chill feeling creeping up through them to the rest of her. Better to bear it alone, till she could do something to make it stop. Anything. She had to make it stop.

Irene told her about The Gigglers. Two bedrooms and a small sitting room they had in the Nanny Flat. Nice view of the lilacs in the spring. The bathroom wanted sorting, but the kitchen wasn't bad, just narrow. Did Ruth know anyone who'd want to live this far out from the town, if the rent was right? Ruth did.

Lily was walking her garden with a palette eye, stopping, and staring from time to time with her hands on her hips, doing her envisioning – seeing one color melt into the next, wanting nothing to jolt, or snag. She is checking the flow, advancing the garden through the months in her mind. She is reviewing the weld of her own work with the existing structures and plants. This garden, called *Lily's* now by all at Motthoe, is not hers, she knows. It has bones of its own, bones like she has never dealt with before.

She has tugged and removed the ivy from the garden in

sheets, like giant drapes. The brambleberries have been rolled away in spiky balls, pitched with a long-handled fork from the wheelbarrow onto the bonfire. The nettles have been dug before they've seeded. And, at last released, the skeleton beneath these obstacles has begun to flesh up. Now when Lily stands in the garden barefoot, as she often does, she can feel the life there. Almost feel the earth moving, simmering and bubbling beneath her, ready for the great boiling burst that summer will bring. She could not explain to anyone the way she feels when a garden she has nurtured begins to birth, but anyone of any sensitivity who had ever seen her look at the ground, tend to a plant, pick a flower – asking the plant's pardon first – would know it.

It was this that encouraged people to employ her, to let a stranger – a stranger with no last name, no papers of recommendation, no formal qualifications – a girl, with an open face, but an odd way of dressing and a scruffy means of transport, into their homes. Many of these people had talked to Lily; told her their problems, told her their husbands drank, or their children weren't doing so well in school. Told her she was beautiful and that they were lonely. They told her these things while she buried her hands in the soft welcome of compost with a distant, kind expression that drew confession and did not scold, or advise. Lily the Tiller, unjudging ear to the world. In this garden though, at Motthoe, Lily sometimes felt that someone was listening to her.

She had tended old plots before, cottages where generations had grown their squashes and marrows, gardens where women had seeded sweet-peas in the same spots their grannies had seeded sweet-peas in. But here, as she spoke in her mind to the gardeners who had gardened before her, each of whom had interred some sliver of soul, as she discovered plants she couldn't name, statuary whose history she did not know, stone benches and jig-sawed paving and pretty sunken nooks, as the puzzles of the garden were discovered and solved, she found a love that she could believe was long-lasting. A notion which to Lily had been previously foreign. She began to believe that a lifetime could be spent in these cozy acres, that in this magical confine, she had found a kingdom, with a past and future equally glorious in possibility. And like all lovers, she wanted to know all there was to know about her beloved.

She washed her hands and went up to the house.

Harry's father's library was dark, leathery and musty. In the center of the room a large, oval table was lit by a large, oval hanging light – the lampshade fringe was hanging off in a dejected tail. Lily had the impression that no-one much had ever read   in here. There was a window, but it faced north and even on a day as cloudless as this it afforded little in the way of illumination. Laden bookshelves reached from the floor to the frieze. There was a single low-backed, low-armed chair at one end of the room, carmine once, but, like the carpet, now a grubby sienna; its seat sunk in the middle as if bearing still the faint indent of the last sitter. It was a room entirely lacking in cheer. Unlike the book that Harry had removed from a corner shelf.

The book had been covered with fine dust, like talcum.

Harry had brushed it off with his sleeve. He went back now for another one. Two more, he said. He wiped those with his sleeve, too. Watching from behind, Lily noted that the label of his shirt was sticking out above his collar. The shirt – olive checked, wash-softened – had slipped back rather on his shoulders. It wasn't tucked in. When he reached up, the undone cuffs fell back from his wrists and up his arms. He turned to Lily, jubilant.

'Right,' he said, to the covers of the books. 'That's a good start, I think.'

'It is,' Lily said.

She stood near him. He passed her the last book and she held it in her hands a moment. It was heavy. She put it on the table next to the others. Harry joined her there.

'This one,' he said, 'is the journal, I think. Yes.' He opened the cover, turned two pages by their corners. 'Yes… it is. This one is the journal of the garden. I only remembered about it when you were talking about the statue. It triggered some memory, I suppose, of…Anyway, there you are. It's a log, kept in the sixties by my mother and the then-gardener.' He ran his palm over one of the book's pages like a priest blessing a baby's forehead.

'Yes,' he said, very quietly, talking to himself. 'Yes, that is my mother's handwriting.' There was a pause, a second's crypt quiet before he said to Lily. 'I never knew her. She died when I was three.'

Lily felt unqualified to respond to this and was, in any case, wise not to since Harry had no desire to discuss the matter further.

'It shows the months and the planting,' he says. 'Then

these others are…Well, one precedes it. That's not a log, but it has plans and so forth in it, of all the gardens. And then this last one is a general reference book.' He brushed his hands together, loosening the last of the dust, and grinned at her again. 'Are they any use?' he asked.

Lily was pleased that she did not have to lie to his enthusiasm.

'They're treasure maps,' she said.

'Oh, good. Great.' He lifted his head, looked around. 'So many of the books are damaged,' he said. He lifted a random title, ran the side of his hand over the cover and put it back, cover-side facing, in front of the slot where it had been. 'I should do something about it.' The joy had leeched from his voice and been replaced with something vague, like something coming from underwater. Lily had heard that sound in his voice before, that submerged sound.

'It's a lot, I expect – this house?'

Harry sighed. Toed the rug. 'There's certainly plenty of it.' He smiled at her. 'I used to look out of my bedroom door in the mornings sometimes, when I first came back – after my father died, and think, "Yep, it's still there." Sometimes, I could really imagine that it wouldn't be – that I'd open the door to a nice, neat, two-bedroomed flat and a free day.'

'I'm not sure I can understand,' Lily said, 'why you wouldn't leave…if that was what you really wanted.' Lily suspected that it was not, had divined this understanding from the ether of him, but she wasn't sure if he wanted to talk about this either. She was simply clearing the brush, in case he wanted to head in that direction.

'That's what you've always done, isn't Lily?' he said.

'Leaving.'

Lily paused; it was a fork she hadn't foreseen. She put her hands so far into her pockets that her upper body hunched. 'I have, yes,' she said.

Harry's eyes on her. 'You leave your gardens behind.'

'No garden is ever finished,' Lily said. 'So, it is not a question of abandoning them half-done. I leave, move on, but I do my best to teach folk how to care for them before I go.' Her fingers fiddled with the seams at the bottoms of her pockets, making her hem twitch.

'They can't though, can they?' he said. 'They can't care for them properly.'

Lily retrieved her hands and lifted the largest book, the reference one, and held, shielding, it across her chest.

'They can't do what you do,' Harry said. 'Nobody can.'

Back outdoors, Lily set herself to sowing scabiosa by scattering, turning lightly with the rake afterwards. Lily believed that a gardener ought to leave the planting loose, give nature the chance to make the picture right. That was why she didn't favor dense plants – hebes or hostas. She liked her gardens to wave, loved to see the delphiniums bobbing their belled spikes in a breeze. Even lavender was a little compact for her taste, but forgiven for its foliage's silver hints and generous fragrance. The variety – *Papillon* – already tilled at Motthoe, was a clue to Harry's mother's similar preferences, confirmed by the notebooks.

Lily found this new knowledge enormously pleasing, but it

was not enough to quell completely the ruffled sensation that she had carried out with her from the house. She kept on – busying it away, making the leftover ends of the ribbons that had tied the daffodils for market into bird-scarers. Soon, pastel streamers were snapping from strings and pea sticks, a cool wind had come up. She lifted her eyes to the sky, she would welcome some rain, but she shook now, knowing it wasn't the weather that was responsible for the feeling inside her.

It was butterflies she thought of – Red Cardinals, something strong in the wing beat. It was an undeniable, skittery feeling, low on the left of her belly. Butterflies. She let her hand rest a moment on the belly butterfly, but it did not flutter again. She passed her palm slowly over her own flank, as if to soothe it, and a lullaby came to her, a snatch of one anyway...*Before the bough breaks*. A few feet away a real butterfly landed on the incipient petal of a snow drop anemone.

Mariposa. He had told her that. It was the Spanish word for butterfly. He had told her that the night they had made this one. It wasn't a night that she had difficulty recalling. Lily's love life, like desert wildflowers, unfolded only rarely, and, while the dazzle of these incidents was bright, it waned fast. Her appetite for physical love was deadened quickly and entirely by familiarity. And memory.

The man, as striking looking as he was mild-mannered, and young, younger than Lily, had been pitching a tent in a wood when she had come across him. It was cold and he had asked her if she thought it safe to light a fire. She had thought it would be, if laid right, a small one. He had worn a fisherman's sweater and a waxed jacket and spoken fluent, but careful English. His hair was black. It had curled a little, behind his ears.

Now he was gone and that was no source of grief for Lily, despite that she now knew, or at least admitted, that their meeting – their aptly outdoor pairing – would have a lifetime's consequences. That the weeks of nascent nausea and queasy aversion to the smell of Irene's good coffee, that the draining weariness, and tetchy feeling around her heart had been the beginning of this – the butterfly spreading inside her. Mariposa she named her – for the cocoon period at least, which would last…She tapped out on her fingers – till October. October – month of exuberant leaf color and branches heavy with pears. Her own butterfly fattened by then. She stood, rickety, and headed for the greenhouse. She was tired, tired in her bones, her eyelids were weighted.

The warmth today had not grown oppressive, the greenhouse was only kindly warm. She lay down on a mound of burlap. She adjusted a hip, and in that instant felt as blossoming as a pea pod. She smiled, feeling better now she was supported. The thinness that the draining worry and denial had wrought was gone. She was a great portly thing, a thing of promise, a fat bud. Her hands both went back to her belly and lay there either side exaggerating the fullness that only she could see. A baby, a child, a daughter – it seemed to her that the baby would be a girl, as sure as an apple tree produces an apple. She was filled with it. A Spanish daughter. Her leaded eyelids pulled her down and she slept.

When Lily woke her body was covered in a sheen of perspiration and all the romance of her falling asleep had gone. The sickness she had suffered so far had been nagging, but never overwhelming, but now it hit her like a severed tree trunk. She lay stiff in case any movement jolted her into wretched heaving. As the waves of alternating hot and cold ran through her, the beflowered previous moments of happiness – at the thought of a child of her own – vanished like the sun behind a snow cloud and was displaced by the dread notion of herself trapped by pregnancy, and parenthood. She vowed, lying there, to set her head against it. To ignore her condition for now. To overcome it by mind as she had other things. Not to think of it again until she was better… equipped. Until she could think of what to think. Of what to do.

There are some stories for which the blank page makes a better audience than the intended one. Ruth sat at her dining room table in the little house her marriage had bought, and wrote hers without hesitation, on a piece of paper torn from a jotter that she had bought for Ashley (previous term's stationery list: A4 pads, red and blue pens, ruler, protractor) that had never been used. The page Ruth had torn out was the back page, the last one, which might have seemed fitting if Ruth had been the sort to sit about pondering symbolism. She wasn't. Ruth knew what she had to do and she was doing it. This was the way she had conducted most of her life. And, if she had got off course some for a while, lost her bearings, she had found her North again now. She had known what she had to do when she had seen Jess set that humility on a plate before her father, known the choice was made when she was sitting alone nursing her injured fingers. They were united, her daughters and her, and they could grow from the collapse of the family they had been, into a new one; something converted, more suited to its environment.

At the side of the house Ruth's car was filled with the last of Jess's and Ashley's things; their rooms were bare. She had already taken one trip to Motthoe that morning, after she had dropped them at school. They had agreed to the move more calmly than she had thought they would. There was a change in them, a setting against their dad that Ruth had not wanted to see, and yet welcomed in the present circumstances as easing her way. Moving them. She had not packed much for herself. She didn't need much and, in any case, did not want things to which memories were attached. Nor had she come to any decision about whether she would come back here again. She was just dealing with Now, with what was in front of her.

The letter she wrote surprised her by being a love letter; loving, at least, a goodbye that had no bitter in it. She put the jotter page into an envelope and wondered where to leave it. In the end she settled on the bed. She had changed the bed linen after she had finished packing, washed the old set and left it to dry. A person could do these things for the man they had been married to, had known since almost boyhood and had borne children to. The man who had held her waist at her mother's funeral. Ruth put the envelope down just as her resolve began to stumble. She took a resolute breath of air that already felt shut-in and walked out.

CHAPTER FIVE

No matter the circumstances of birthplace (in Lily's case the unloading bay outside Cherriford A&E) the heart has its own preferred dwelling. Lily was a girl of the earth rather than the asphalt of her early life, and, more than that, of the country. She had come in her edge-of-village adult years to understand some of its ways and so she did not flinch when she heard, echoed from some distance by a trick of the land contours, the thudding sound of a shot: Ogden, or Dan shooting for the pot. What was interesting about this was that it was as likely to be Dan. He had a heart in the fields, too. He could ride, she'd heard from Ruth. He could shoot and he had a feel for weather, for seasons. It was him the dogs looked to for walks. Now, as the echo died away, she watched the rabbits, who had been sitting fatly at the grassy wood-side, fleeing to their burrows and made mental note to ask Ogden to erect some higher stands for the seedling pots, lest the creatures, who she loved to see in the mornings, make short work of her baby plants at night. It was a question of circles; loved and loathed, life and death. Eater and eaten. All part of the weave of the land.

Irene; down for her daily catch-up, is looking worn. She is. The skin under her eyes is pouched and her lips are pale. There is a faint stain on the left leg of her trousers – the same trousers she has worn for the past two days.

'Third bad night with mother,' she says.

Both of them are bleary eyed, but Lily's bodily trials (which is how, for the moment, she is thinking of her pregnancy) are disguised, buried by beauty. In fact, the luminous quality of her face is exaggerated lately by a slight weight loss which has chiseled her cheekbones further toward Ethereal. Irene, though no longer stunned by her, is nevertheless still faintly awed that a human can look the way that Lily does – inhumanly exquisite. They sit sipping from their cups in companionable quiet till Irene brightens up and tells Lily that Harry has decided to sell one patch of land up at the riverside to a fella who's been asking to buy it for two years – who wants to set up home there and live from fishing licenses. Harry says also: get a decent builder in, do a proper job on the two empty cottages by the lane gate. Find tenants, make a plan for the rents.

'Feet feeling for the ground, then,' says Lily.

'We'll see if they reach,' says Irene. And she laughs. She is hoping the fishing fella calls back quick before Harry reverts to hoping things along, doing everything the hazy hard way. She has called a builder in the town and arranged to meet him at the cottages; 3:15 today, for a walkover and a quote. She is looking forward to the project. Something to get her teeth into.

Irene parked her car in front of the first of the two cottages. They are joined at a central wall, but the arrangement is such that the second one is accessed via a gate at the side and has no driveway of its own. The cottages are a hundred and seventy years old – new by Motthoe standards.

The Builder was already there. He had a lorry with Connor Co – Builders written on the side of it in black letters. It had muddy wheels and one of the rear doors was open. The Builder was standing outside the front cottage wearing a dark blue sleeveless puffer jacket over his jeans, talking on his telephone. His chin was tucked into the curve of the jacket collar. When he saw Irene, he looked up and smiled and hung up on whomever he had been talking to. Irene wondered who it was.

'Hello,' he said.

Irene had her little notebook with her and she carried it in her hand along with the cottage keys. The Builder stood back to let her pass ahead of him onto the narrow porch to unlock the door – a formality, half the windows fittings were hanging loose. They stepped onto a pile of junk mail – addressed to The Householder – and a load of free newspapers and a lot of leaflets for pizza deliveries. The Builder bent and picked these up and stacked them on the mantelpiece in the small front room. That was when Irene began to like him, but she didn't know it yet.

The Builder ran his eyes over the front room and walked to a door on the other side of it. He leaned his upper, puffer-jacketed half through the far door with one hand on the jamb. Then he ducked back to Irene again.

'What did you have in mind?' he said.

Irene thought he had long legs. 'It'll be for renting,' she said.

'Right.' His eyes ran up, over the walls, across the ceiling, down again along the skirting.

Irene raised a hand, gesturing for him to go on through the door that separated the room they were in from the one behind. He went through, leaned into the fireplace and peered up the chimney, did that thing again, the knowing scan. Beyond them was the kitchen. He looked at that, then came back towards her, and went up the stairs as if she wasn't there – he took them two at a time. Irene followed – self-conscious up there with him. The ceilings were lower, the spaces more intimate, despite their emptiness. She pulled herself inward and hunched her shoulders. The Builder didn't seem to notice. He ducked under a beam when he bent to check the window fastenings.

'Ladder's in the van,' he said. He grinned at her and

side-stepped past her to go back down the stairs, jumped the last three. He climbed into the roof space with a flashlight. Irene could see the beam of it crossing the hatch, then his feet, booted, dropped back out. So easy, such a fit in his skin.

'Joists are fine,' he said. 'And the roof's not bad.'

'Goodo,' she said. And wished she hadn't, wished she'd just nodded and made a stab at looking intelligent.

They stood out front after Irene had locked the door again. It was less rattling than being inside together. Although, probably, it was only Irene who felt that way. It was.

His name was Nick, Nick Connor. It fitted him as well as the rest of him did. Straightforward type, not the sort to divert his gaze – from subsidence, or blushes. Fifty-odd. Hair graying, silvering in sunlight. Strong-looking. Irene put her hand in her pocket and fetched out her car key. Then she hid it in her palm because the key ring – lurid orange, cracked plastic, emblazoned with a shouty promotion for a cab company – seemed ugly all of a sudden, and twee, and not just useful the way it had seemed before.

'I'll write it up and get an estimate to you by the end of the week,' he said. He walked her to her car and opened the door for her to get in.

Irene tucked her gilet around herself and thanked him. She had to drive off first so that he could turn. He was looking up at the cottage roof as she did, and then, when she checked the rear vision, he had taken the phone back out of his jacket and tucked it to his ear.

Irene put the radio on in her car, feeling something inside of herself, underneath the ribbed knit of her spring-weight jumper, right down under her vest. She felt something. But she did not know that her life had changed.

At Motthoe Harry said, 'Seen the builder then?'

'Yes,' she told him.

'What's he said?'

'All fine,' she said. 'General refit and some damp to be dealt with.'

She sounded vague. Harry wondered should he have gone himself.

After she has talked to Harry, Irene goes back to Lily's garden, where she can enjoy not thinking. Where Lily will put her to some helpful, non-taxing work that will tug a temporary veil over her Mother Worries and other unsettlings until going-home time .

But before that: *The grass boy*: Leggy and callow-skinned, with a baseball cap touting a city he's never been to, in a country he's never been to, shading his eyes, though it is overcast and past four.

He walks to the door, back of the kitchen, ducked the capped head through it, like a bird – pecky left, then right. Nobody. No matter. Out beyond, in a small building, behind the laundry, he pulls back the winter cover from his machine. Dan has serviced it and tanked it up. Dan, thinks the boy, is all right – understands machines, doesn't talk at you, gets things done. Old Lord Harry though… Lord Harry of Dreams is worse than the women for talking. Wants your ideas. Wants your company.

The boy – not a boy now, eighteen this summer, College – maneuvres the machine out onto the level patch of concrete in front of the opened double doors, feels the surge of contentment as he mounts and fires the ignition. The wall of engine noise closing around him. Inside, sealed, he has the controls.

He will start at the front.

The mower noise – settled to a low purr, the noise of summer, of Saturdays, the noise of the smell of meandering afternoons – floats up and over the wall to Irene and Lily.

'Jason,' Irene says to Lily.

Irene puts down her trowel – tenacious little tool – and a look comes over her.

Lily lifts a brow.

'I need to talk to him,' she says and stands heavily.

'We could sell more planters,' Lily suggests. Guessing Irene's worries are money-based. Worries so often are.

'That'll do for Ruth, a month or two longer. But Harry and Dan can manage the grass. The boy was a luxury – a favor to his father. G.P. in the town. Played in boyhood with Harry.'

Lily nods. Lily knows.

Jason cuts the engine when he sees Irene walking towards him across the unmown section, but not immediately. He tips his cap back some, because he's a good boy, with good parents. Then puts his hands back, light on the dinky mower steering wheel, ready for a swift end to the interruption.

'Jason…'

"Llo.' Baritone. The man emerging.

'Father and mother fine?' Irene asks, coming to him, oiling the way to her unwanted task.

'Fine,' says Jason. Fingers drum, drumming on the dinky steering wheel.

'Jason…' Big Breath in.

She looks different, thinks Jason. Less sickly.

'Jason,' she says. 'I'm not sure we'll be able to pay you this summer.' Make it plain. Cruel otherwise.

Jason, silent a moment, chews his bottom lip. Otherwise, relaxed.

'All right,' he says. Nods. Pulls the cap back down. Hits the starter. Turns the machine in a careful arc and picks up where he left off. Up and down easy, even rows striped.

Irene watches his back and realizes for the first time that he is there, as she is – for something beyond. Caught in the net of the world that is Motthoe, but not struggling.

Behind the wall Lily has heard the engine restart and she has guessed it too.

Jason continues up and turning, down and turning – uniform and restful as the waves of an incoming tide on a windless day. Till he reaches the long stretch of the Italian Garden – still called, though living now in the dim of its own shadow. Then he slows and almost jerks to a stop. Cuts the engine, leaving a deeper silence than ever existed before he started it. He has caught the view through the door to the old walled garden and glimpsed there the first months' work; the tidied pathways, repaired and debris cleared. Willow panels boxing in the end of each border, planters uprighted and tulip filled. Twigs and shambolics cut back. Climbing roses tied in. Hand painted labels marking the summer-flowering bulbs. Narcissi riotous at the back where the woods begin, and sumptuous despite its late and light cutting back, the abundant white clematis.

'Armandii,' says Lily, come to the gate to examine the silence.

Jason, unsure momentarily, doesn't respond.

'The clematis,' Lily says and turns in the direction he is facing and extends her arm, not quite pointing, but indicating the sprawl of it. '"Traveller's Joy" in some cultures.'

Jason, a half-gardener for a mother – loves her window boxes, grows tomatoes in tubs – understands 'clematis' and nods.

'I'm Lily,' Lily says turning to him. 'You're Jason, then.'

'I am,' he admits.

She waits.

'You've done some work,' he says.

'I've done some work,' she agrees.

He walks with her to the gate and through it. Irene is on her knees at the far end with a trowel, happily weeding. Seed packets – poppies and nigella tumbled on the bench – slats replaced and painted – next to her. That's it then, thinks Jason, it was a bit of toil that toned her up. He walks on through and then out the rear corner and down the path to the greenhouse – hospital sorted, unfamiliar. Rows of trays. Water butts on the down pipes. Panes all repaired and sealing the world out, all within lulled.

'Need any help?' asks Jason turning to Lily behind.

'Always,' says Lily as, distantly, the phone in Irene's pocket begins to buzz like an insistent hornet.

'How bad is she?' Irene asks, but she already knows because the village woman never calls without provocation.

One week later at 5:15 in the evening Lily is sitting, not her usual style, at the kitchen table worrying at the index finger of her left hand with an eye tooth.

'My mother would mustard that finger,' Irene says.

Outside, the sky is raging dark. Ruth flips a light switch and the flickering neon strip – added for convenience in 1982 – sputters and steadies and brightens the kitchen. One, side-lying, Labrador lifts his head, looks up and begins to quiver, but Ruth makes a noise that soothes him and he goes back to his chase-filled dreams. In the first floor sitting room with the tartan rugs, Harry is watching television with Ruth's girls who have forgotten their homework projects in favor of the headlines – Storms: hard rain and fearful nights coming.

'Hail is worst,' says Lily. Standing at the sink and leaning over it, two hands bracing herself at the counter, looking out and up at the sky.

Dan, coming into the kitchen, sneaking up on the camaraderie there via the second entry says: 'For the garden?'

'Yes,' she says, not turning. 'Hail is the worst.'

Ruth pours tea for Dan as the servants' bell above the Aga peals.

Ruth pours more tea. 'Take her this,' she says to Irene.

Irene is already on her feet. Ready to go see what Mother wants.

It had taken Dan and Harry and Ogden and Jason to move Irene and Mother up to Motthoe. Jason shifting the tractor trailer expertly down the main road in contravention of half a dozen by-laws; 24 mph, fifteen cars at rear as he took the last left at the edge-of-town roundabout, trailer hitched behind. They had nestled Mother in the back seat of Harry's car – Ogden carrying her to it like she was a princess, Irene in beside her with three light blankets and a towel and bowl in case of incidents – none of which occurred.

Mother, who had griped and whimpered at Irene for twenty-two years looked her straight in the eye when Irene told her that they were invited to move to Motthoe for a month or two, so that Irene could keep working, and she said, 'Motthoe...yes.'

Just like that, a straight-up affirmative, unblemished by grizzle or complaint. Then she had settled back on her pillows and taken her cod liver oil capsule with three swallows from a full glass of orange juice and smiled. Smiled.

Irene, the air coming out of her so that she felt she might liquefy, or levitate, the weight released from her...could not believe it.

'We'll live at Motthoe for a while then, shall we Mother?' she confirmed, still assuming the worst – that The Positive would be torn off her again, ripped away like a wound dressing.

But...'Yes. We will live at Motthoe,' said mother. Then she went to sleep, with a face on her that told of the sweetest of dreams and she did not disturb Irene once during the night.

This turn of events, like all the best ones, had come about simply, when Irene, coming home to find Mother sitting up, but extremely crotchety after the neighbor woman's call, had telephoned Harry to say she would not be back that afternoon. When she had been summoned home again the next day, she had said to Harry that relying on her in the short-term might not be wise. And Harry had looked up, easy as you like and said: 'Why don't you both just move up here for a bit, that way you're not worrying.'

As if it were that straightforward. As if her mother would agree to such a thing. As if life could just get manageable, and almost merry, overnight. It had.

Dan and Ogden, quick to projects these days, had rejigged the old servants' bell in the bedroom that had been Harry's mother's – Harry's parents had loved one another, but on traditional, mutually respectful terms. The room had been undisturbed for years and, like everything at Motthoe that had been Harry's mother's, was in better nick than most of the house, as if those sensitive fingers had continued to stroke the smooth surfaces. The room was on the first floor – outlook over the front garden and the now dry lake beyond and the sea beyond that. There was a damp patch, grubby gold in one upper corner, but not bad. The bed was a blonde mahogany half-tester. Ruth had stripped and scrubbed the soft furnishings. Mother's own small dresser had come up in the horse trailer and Lily had filled the room with pink peonies so fat that, at first, Irene held her breath, thinking her mother would complain at their voluptuous drooping – some were already littering their surrounds with petal debris.

But mother had said: 'Peonies', under her breath, gently, as if remembering something, and chosen not to go straight to bed despite the tire of her trip up the hill and the gaudy assault on her eyeballs by the driveway azaleas, now in full, violent bloom. She sat, instead, in a button-backed nursing chair, turned to the high front window, and peered out, remembering, remembering, something more.

Now when Irene hands her the cup she says: 'A storm's coming.'

'Yes,' says Irene. 'Lily's fretting for her flowers.'

Irene's mother nods, yes, and sips her tea and does not complain that it is cold.

Downstairs Lily, turning into the room, restless there and wanting back to the greenhouse, looked at her worn finger, mousey bitten down beyond the tip, the one that gave her away, then lifted her own tea. Pink she noted, rosehip. It was bought regularly now, especially for her. The warmth she felt, drinking it, came not from the pot, but from the sharing. From the generosity of these women, each with her own troubles. The whole spring sky came back to her fleetingly and was reflected in the smile she gave them.

'Wouldn't have picked you for a nail nibbler,' Ruth said, giving her the look – the mother-of-teenage-girls-look, the what's-behind-this look. Seeing through her.

'Everyone's got a closet,' Lily said. 'Something in it mostly.'

When it does come, almost exactly forty-eight hours later, the storm does not announce itself, does not rattle the gate lightly for warning, nor tread squarely up the path...tap tap tap, here I come. Instead, an iron shadow of volcano cloud looms as if directly spewed upwards from the sea and bursts off a tremendous whamming crack that rattles the ground and the house and all within it. One of the dogs, yippy already with thunder warning, whining and clawing an imaginary hole in the kitchen slate, lets forth a screaming howl and doubles his efforts.

Lily, who has spent the afternoon armoring her garden

from every peril she can foresee, flaps to the kitchen window where she is once again stationed and sees immediately that her efforts will provide puny defense. She moves now to the door, out through the porch, past the old scullery door, down the four curved steps, running, her feet bare, the break, the storm ahead of her. She is running into it. The wind, which has caught the old hinge of the garden door is whipping up tremendous and is already lifting the tail ends of the poly-tunnels she has fixed over her babies.

Behind her come running: Jess, who has wept her bitter Boy Tears in that garden, and felt them drain. And Ashley, who loves Lily and has had as much fun (who knew) bedding up annuals, earth beneath her nails, as she ever had hanging around out back of the mall hoping one of her sister's discarded boys might give her a look. And Ruth, who has seen there, under Lily's compassionate eye, her own dear girls as they can be, as they really are – hardworking and funny and kind.

Behind Ruth come: Irene, who has laughed in that garden, more than she's laughed since she can't remember, and there found her first beautiful friend. And Dan, who has, sometimes at night lately sat on the bench that Lily has had installed there for contemplation and contemplated. And then Harry, who has seen one small, snapped-off piece of his dreams come to fruit there. All of them racing, all of them calling out over the wind roar. All half entwined by calamity and chaos.

But then: Ogden.

Ogden, voice for open ground, command for animals and machines, having sensed the weather early, having seen the village church flag turn to the north, and battened what needs to be battened on the farm, has come to the house, drawn to young Lily and her projects – the projects that have, for the first time since Mary's death given his evenings purpose, has come to help. He stations himself at the gate and booms, above the rain, above the wind, over the panic and through the lashing hair and toppling garden furniture. Commander Ogden. And through him Order. All that can be is tied off, re-battened, protected more and bedded further against the gale and wet coming sideways now and stinging, ripping at exposed leaves and furious pounding the last of the pendulous peony heads.

Harry, fighting with a flapping trellis end and losing, feels the allied pair of Ogden and Dan take either side of it and relieve him of the task, which they complete efficiently. He stands for a moment, unneeded, arms at his sides before turning to find some job he is up to, but by then, everything is in hand. He stands in the rain, arms at his sides, unneeded on his own ship – he cannot captain it.

Inside, apart from all this raging energy, Irene's mother rings her bell, and rings and rings it. Nobody hears.

Irene's mother stops ringing the bell.

What a hurley-burley when they all come in, dripping, laughing, hoping for the best. Lily pitching herself back up to the window, though she can't see the garden from there, pitching herself up nevertheless, gazing in its direction, like a mother through a school gate. Ruth pulls the kettle onto the hot Aga element and Irene goes off to check on Mother.

Irene's eyes swept Mother's room, and then the adjoining room where she has slept herself these past nights on a cot

119

bed – Harry's mother's dressing room.

'*Mother?*' she calls. '*Mother?*'

Irene rushes to the kitchen and sends them all clattering off in turmoil again, down the hallways. Behind them the kettle, beginning to steam, shrieks and whistles.

It is Harry who finds Mother. Irene in her panic has not noticed that the walking frame, hitherto parked beside an unplumbed washstand, is no longer there. Harry – who has absented himself from the kitchen's jolly, job-well-done atmosphere – hears the rub of its wheels on the tiled floor at the back of the gun room. She has descended to the ground floor, extremely slowly and rather majestically, in a tiny rear elevator – installed for Harry's grandfather.

'Hello,' says Harry.

Mother barely glances at him – got something on her mind and heading to scratch it. Clippety-clip along the passage. Harry's thinking: never wake a sleepwalker. But then she stops and whips her titchy head – bun at the nape fixed by Irene mornings – whips it left to right, left to right. *Aah*, she decides, *left*. She opens a door that hasn't been opened six times in as many years and enters. She rounds a large table in the center of the room and trots along to the back wall, right side.

Harry, catching up, standing next to her, looking at the wall as she is, waits. Never wake a sleepwalker. He stands beside her, quite silent, until the tight centre spring of her gives way and, in its uncoiling, she smiles. A shiny little smile like a sequin. Her pointed hand rises from the walking frame, on which she has made progress sharp enough for Harry, the docile walker, the ruminator, to have to pick up pace to get abreast of her.

'There…' she says, revealing a secret.

Harry looks…trying to see it…nothing. A hole in the wall, a set of holes in the wall. Cousins to many more holes in these walls and many larger.

'The dart board,' she says, sequined all over now. She lowers her hand. 'Your father hammered in the nail, bang, bang, bang and we watched. All the children; evacuees. Pasty London faces, they had. Never eaten cream. Never seen the sea. All watching with those pasty townie faces while your father hammers up the dart board. And then we played. We just flung the darts willy-nilly, till we got the hang of it… and made these holes in the wall.' She leans forward on the walker and Harry figures her for fully awake now, and not at risk therefore, and offers to get her a chair.

She declines by waggling her head. 'And all through the months after,' she says to the wall. 'I came up with my mother, she made beds and porridge….Forty children there were here. Two sets with their mums – both gave birth here. But one of the babies died. She was six months old, her name was Annie. Chubby thing, she was, grin like a cherub. Something wrong with her heart. Your father carried the coffin. White it was. Not a proper coffin, an apple box, painted. No tiny coffins to be had, war years. Your father carried it down the aisle, covered in daisies we'd collected from the meadow at Curston Farm. He carried it on his shoulder. He was a lad still, but doing man's work because the fighting took the men…it took my father and my brother. Your father, just a lad, walked down that aisle in his best suit – too small and none new to be had – with that white box covered in daisies on his right shoulder and his left arm up across supporting it. Solemn as winter, he was. Held all his tears for the dead baby and the poor, crazed mother – held them back, like a man. Like the brave man he was. Your grandfather was away fighting, and your dad was here at Motthoe. Thirteen years old or thereabouts, your Dad was then. Doing a man's work. We all looked up to him.'

They stand a moment, each alone with their thoughts, and then the old lady begins, in the high wind instrument voice of an old lady raised on proper hymns, to sing *'Abide with Me'*...a splintery warble...*'Fast falls the eventide'*.

In that room of neglect among many, the room where a newspaper, abandoned in 1964 still sits under a chair which lacks upholstery, Harry stares at the wall and sees the holes there and tries, in them, to see a father he never knew.

'There's a tree down,' the old lady says – zipping from wool-gathering to cognizance with rubber band alacrity. Alacrity enough to startle any man, let alone dazed Harry, who turns to her dumb.

'Hmm..?' says Harry. A slow rally.

'Tree down,' she answers, brusque, flicking her walker round like a conductor's baton. 'Top of the driveway. Blocked it all across. I rang my bell, but nobody came.'

'We were sorting the garden,' Harry said, taking up behind her.

'Best sort the tree now,' she says.

She says it again in the kitchen, which, finding herself on the ground floor, she heads for like she's been doing it all her life. Harry, as ever, on the follow.

'Mother!' says Irene, one hand flapping to her chest, just

then about to convene a search of the grounds. 'I've been all over looking for you.'

Mother, now established in a chestnut leather chair that will become hers, says, 'Nobody came. I rang and rang.' *Dying on the floor, I was... might have been...* her tone says to Irene.

'I was that worried,' says Irene. She takes a seat, with an involuntary give out of breath and knees; dumps into it. 'That worried,' she says again. Her breath is coming in sprinter's puffs.

Ruth pours her some tea.

Mother already has tea. She lifts the cup to her tortoise lips, saucer balanced in her spare hand (Ruth has fetched out the porcelain for her.) 'First cup I've had that was hot,' says Mother.

She has improved since moving to Motthoe, but not so much yet that she can completely extricate a barb from a blessing.

Harry held out his hands, lifted them and turned them over. Veins were beginning to stand up on the backs of them now, the nails were square, but he had long fingers – pianist's fingers. They'd come from his mother, those hands. As it happened, he had her ear for music too, but he indulged it rarely. Harry's days were spent, not in creation, not even in construction, just in propping things up. He felt sometimes like a wafery version of Samson, one arm outstretched either side, or a puny Hercules, Motthoe on his back. He wasn't up to it – this weight of history. And yet he felt, felt keenly that he must not let his burden go. And, if he did, what then anyway? What would he do? He'd pondered it often enough, the possibility of walking away. He'd tried it. But he was frankly unemployable now, with his useless, piano player's hands.

When he was younger, doing his stint in the military, briefly pleasing his father, loathing his life, Harry had imagined himself a financier. He had friends who'd gone into The City and made money. Two of them were alcoholics now, three were divorced. It didn't seem as shiny to him, that life, as it had. He'd tried traveling, but that had been lonely. Motthoe at least felt like home. And then this spring, since the girl, Lily, the gorgeous girl, had come and fallen in love with the garden – he had recognized her love instantly because it had forced recognition in him of his own attachment to Things Motthoe. Since then, the place, warming to love as all things do, had rewarded them – the garden at least, the walled garden had come back to life.

At night sometimes, watching Lily working for a few intruder moments, Harry had seen not Lily, but his mother. Strange misty images of his mother that he had not been aware of carrying with him all these years, strange, soft, unearthed images of his dead mother working in her garden. The garden that had known only neglect these last years, because Harry's father had eventually lost interest in life outside his room and because Harry, with his pianist hands had been no more use to the garden than he had to the outbuildings and the pipework and the fascias and the soffits. Harry had neither the hands nor head for any of these things and his father had always known it. He had assured himself, for as long as he could summon the energy to do so, that Harry's leanings would grow more practical with age, that he might make money enough to employ the skills of others, but Harry had failed on both counts and here was the evidence around him: plaster cracked and peeling, window frames and skirtings decayed, stonework in ever increasing disrepair.

And yet now; small awakenings, signs of life. The glass in the greenhouse restored. The border walls mended. The leak, under the Belfast sink in the kitchen, plugged (by Ogden, on Ruth's request). Not enough. Not enough – band-aids on a ragged wound – but something at least. Beginnings such as there had not been for a long, long time and yet they filled him, these trifling positives, not always with pleasure, but often with despair at his own ineptness, his lack of ability to do anything himself. He could not build things, make them grow, could not cook or make things. He was Harry, dreamer of dreams and no substance to make them fact. He knew that, knew what they thought of him.

Harry got up now and walked to the music room. He had asked the tuner up and paid the bill himself – with cash so as not to get that look from Irene when she went through the balances. She was a marvel. Irene, and her book-keeping skills, he was aware, had saved Motthoe from sooner and greater ruin, but she gave him a look sometimes that veered uncomfortably from sisterly to schoolgirlish. A look that wanted talk and explanations that he didn't want to provide.

Outside, a night jar sang. Ruth must have opened the French doors that led on to the small, private courtyard, urns in its corners, beginnings of moonlight on the gray stone. Harry did not know it, but his mother used to read in that courtyard. Perhaps her ghost still did, because when Harry closed his eyes and lifted his otherwise useless hands to the keys, when the first mournful drifts of *Clair de Lune* began to lift and sail, something beyond the windows stirred.

CHAPTER SIX

During his first prison stretch, and his inevitable second, and in the times he spent in squats and on the streets between, you would not have picked Seth Banbury for a man who knew the hedgerows, knew the seasons. He had already looked by then like a man who knew only nothingness, or violence. But there had been tranquil points in Seth's life. Periods of closeness, even affection. His Grandad – Pa Joe, traveling man, caravan dweller – had put a hand on Seth's shoulder more than once, had taught him mushrooming and fishing and egg theft. Pa Joe had taught Seth how to trap and how to use a knife. When Seth was six, Pa Joe had taught him, with marble patience, how to skin a rabbit; how to slip the knife point in just above the leg joints – not too deep – and run a single slice up the hide to backside, how to use his hands to slide the skin up from the slimy sinews. These things stood a man in good stead in the moorlands.

It was Pa Joe who had told Seth about America: big country. Hobos in America rode trains, jumped box cars, Pa Joe said; miles and miles to travel, days and days of space. Real freedom that was – big country. Not like this piss-piddling island, where somebody was always up your arse. Not like this piss piddling excuse for a craphole place. Seth still remembered things Pa Joe had said, despite the obliterating elements of his life, the shutting-down parts, and he knew what his grandfather had been talking about when he had longed for The Vast. Seth had walked Britain up and down, side to side, and always come to the doorway of the sea – the heavy, shut doorway. No way off this piss-piddling island.

Lily had never been one for the ocean up close. It was lanes she sought; openness made her vulnerable. But on Sunday, in the minty wake of the storm, the sky had burned up clean and she knew there'd be seaweed lying easy for the harvesting. She had come to the bay to fill her sacks. And it wasn't so bad out there after all. The air, which she could taste, suited her this morning and she liked the feeling on her skin of the breeze off the water. She felt clean. She wasn't alone.

A party had grown up around Lily's mentioning to Ruth that she was going to take the van down to the bay, the chance was too good to miss, seaweed being one of the best and few free fertilizers (comfrey and nettle juice and wood-burner ash besides). In the buzz of activity of the leaving Dan had offered to stay behind and reserve one ear for Mother's Bell. This offer, while fairly curtly conveyed – across the rim of a chipped coffee mug – was clearly sincere, but Irene did not quite believe in it, too many things in her life were lightening, formerly weighty woes evaporating, turning to so much spindrift.

Irene asked Dan was he sure. He was. Irene assured Dan that her mother was sleeping and unlikely to disturb him.

'She'll be fine,' Dan said.

'I'll take my own car. I can be back in twenty minutes, if you need me,' Irene said.

'Fine,' Dan said.

'Her medicines are on the bedside table,' Irene said.

Dan said nothing.

'And there's water there. Although she may want a cup of tea if she wakes…'

Dan said nothing.

'If she does, could you explain that I'll be back soon? I won't stay long. Of course, she may not wake. She's had her breakfast, and often goes back to sleep for an hour or two at this time.'

Dan began to look vexed.

'Here's my number,' Irene said, writing her phone number on the notepad that Ruth kept on the table for lists. She tore off the page and handed it to Dan.

'Fine,' Dan said.

Harry, oblivious, risking the implosion of the entire flimsy arrangement asks, 'Did you not want to come down yourself, then?'

'No.' Mother-sitting is a small price, Dan thinks, for some time alone.

A shadow passes over young Jess's face. She is hanging languorous off the kitchen table with a slice of uncut toast in her hand.

Lily sees the shadow. She has already noted that the girl watches Dan constantly, as if voodoo-drawn, moves herself nearer to him whenever possible, but she has seen in Dan no corresponding response to this behavior, not even a faint marking of it. Not yet. She will bide her time for now, in case he does. She will be ready.

They drove in convoy. Down the driveway, across the main road and down again, another, steeper lane that led to the sea. Lily worried for the van's undersides – Ruth's girls inside, squealing at the lurches – but bar a rock scrape or two, they had made it to the flat area above the beach that served as a car park and picnic area, and a smoking and love-making spot, as required. Today it was empty. Except now for Lily's van and Irene's saloon, and after that the Motthoe jeep, Harry at the wheel.

As soon as they had stopped the girls leaped out and ran and scrambled down onto the sand, shoeless, wild running as horses. Lily stood a moment in the safety of the lea of the cars, and looked around, up and over, as she always did. Irene, joining her, followed her eye line to the farmland behind them.

'Once it was all Motthoe,' she said.

Lily, whose thoughts had been moving in another direction took a moment to catch the thread.

'Lost in a card game,' Irene said. 'Or a duel, depending who's doing the telling, and when.' She smiles. 'Lost anyway, or sold more like, some time back, a hundred years, more. Motthoe is divorced from its land, Harry says. And that is its tragedy.'

'Is it?' says Lily.

'He means that the house can't sustain itself without enough farmland. There's too little income to pay for the upkeep.'

Lily looked about again; at the richness, the cushiony hills dipping to the sea. She saw colors, shapes, texture, not economy. Taking in the landscape now, Motthoe's landscape, she could understand how someone could love it. Irene clearly did, almost as much as Harry. But she, Lily, must not. There was no history to be made here for her. She was a nomad. She had to be.

Lily shook her head from thoughts and smiled at Irene and handed her a bucket.

'Dip whatever you find in the sea and only take it if it smells good. Just the top layer,' she said.

Ruth lined up with Harry. Each took their pail, or sack and followed where Ruth's girls had gone, down a steep, gorse-lined track that opened out to a dune. Gulls screamed above them. They sounded like Ashley and Jess.

'How will you use it?' Harry said. He was walking the water line, wavelets licking his feet.

Lily told him about the potash in the kelp – useful at this time of year when the wood burners weren't much used. She

told him how he could dig seaweed into the compost heap
to help the breakdown of the soil.

She is a marvel, Harry thought. Or rather, this constant
thought, turning and repeating in perpetual hum, voiced
itself again with pointed clarity. *And all that's best of dark and
bright*, he thinks.

'Hoo doo, Dozy.' Softly called from the sliding doorway of
the greenhouse where Lily had fallen asleep after the sacks
of seaweed had been emptied and sorted. Ruth stood for a
moment as if asking permission to enter.

Lily opened her eyes more fully. It seemed this was
invitation enough.

In Ruth came, a tray in her hand with a jug on it – Irene's
mother's elderflower. Lemon slices in it. 'I thought you might
be thirsty after your nap.' Ruth said, setting the tray on a
work top, brushing compost from it, moving aside a small
tower of stacked seedling pots. 'Wears everybody out, sea
air,' she said, seeming not to require responses. She poured a
glass of cordial for Lily and handed it to her.

Lily took the glass. Her skin still felt tight from salt and
wind. Her stomach was rocking. She sipped the cordial, all
tentativeness.

When Ruth had seen Lily drink a little, she passed her a
small plate of biscuits – ginger. Ruth's manner, permanently
motherly, allowed for no refusal, so Lily took a biscuit and ate
it, lips closing nibbly over the crisp edge. She was surprised
that it made her feel better.

Funny, Ruth thought, that moment that changed Not Knowing to Knowing. The moment that changed things. One minute a thing was one way, a person was, and next moment it was all different. No way to tell exactly how it was you Knew, you just did. Intuition. Ruth had seen Lily's baby sure as if Lily had held it up to her. What was it then? Her face a little different maybe, the bust and belly on her. Not so you'd notice, not particularly, especially given those baggy articles she dressed in. Maybe that was why? Trying to hide it. Ruth was in no doubt that the baby was a secret. She would not bring it up with Lily, if Lily said nothing first. She'd see the girl looked after, though. Try to get her to eat something. The kipping…now that made more sense. Still, she'd had the impression that Lily's sleeping habits may have always been unusual. Well, they seemed unusual to Ruth, nodding off in the green house and keeping strange hours at night – Dan said he'd seen her in the garden in the dark. Barefoot, too. Prowling about like a fox. Anyway, Ruth had the impression that those were not just pregnancy hours.

Ruth thought maybe the pacing, and the night wakefulness, was rooted in something different. Something mysterious, or furtive, fearful even. At first Ruth had found this side to Lily, the lack of openness, off-putting. Ruth being one for the heart-on-the-sleeve till recent times. But now, lately, she'd learned something – open books were fine when life was trundling along, more or less in a predictable direction. But it was different when things took a negative turn. Ruth had talked to no one about Rob; about the drinking and the not-coming-home nights. Ruth had told no one that it wasn't what it was any more. That her marriage had crumbled, and she nearly with it. Ruth didn't tell people she cried at night, so why should Lily tell them she paced. One thing about a little hardship, it soon softened your antlers. Or it should, at least – should make you go easier on others' invisible burdens. We don't none of us know what anyone else is carrying around with them, she thought, reaching the house, taking the rear door inside.

Ruth passed the old corridor to the larder and the pantry, went into the kitchen where the Aga ticked with heating despite the season. She rinsed the elderflower jug and put the lemon slices in the bin for Lily's compost. Washed the glasses, and the plate of its biscuit crumbs. Wiped the tray and slid it into the rack. Lily's baby. Was that a heartache then, unwanted? *Aah*, thought Ruth, *surely not*; Ruth had a great faith in babies to turn things around. Not that she was naive. She'd seen folks have them who shouldn't have, seen selfish, irresponsible and just plain ignorant parents make a hash of things, but on the whole she believed in a child's power to make a parent. She wanted to believe it.

Ruth put her two hands on the old wooden part of the counter top, beside the Belfast sink, wiping cloth still in one, and stared out the small window above. There'd have been no window there once. Once the cooks and kitchen maids, the workers like her would have had no view from the kitchen, just their work to focus on. She often thought of those things, the lives that had preceded hers, the cleaning that had preceded hers, as she went about her duties at Motthoe. Different thing then it would have been, for the likes of Lily. No husband and a baby coming. Not all change is bad, she thought. How would life have been for her back along, a century before, or more? No, some things had changed for the better. And life here at Motthoe would not be so bad for Lily and her child. She could work in the garden some, live for next to nothing and grow her own food. Send the tot to the infants' school at Moorstead, go to playgroup at the church. Ruth felt a twinge of jealousy, a sharp longing for the years of *The Wheels on the Bus*. She'd taken Jess to the library in the town on Thursday mornings, every Thursday morning till she was three, sat her daughter on her lap and worked her pudding hands, singing along with the other mums: *the wheels on the bus go round and round*. Jess rotating her fat elbows in time to the tune. Like it was yesterday, you said, if you ran into one if the other old-days mums outside the supermarket, teenagers in tow. You felt like it was a million years ago. You'd ask after each other's kids: what they were doing, how they were getting on, and you'd both say, Fine, and add some titbit – usually comic. Nobody ever said they cried at night.

Everyone's got a closet.

Irene had kept her secret, not told anyone where she was going. She had imagined that she never would tell anyone where she had been. She could barely tell herself. For the second time in a week her mother was being cared for by someone else, and this time at night, well, evening at least – a first. For the second time Irene had passed on The Instructions; for her mother's pills, her needs and done some guilty pillow-plumping before she'd left, checked and checked again…You'll be all right, Mother? The assurance tonight had come from Mother's own dry lips. Yes, she would be; no attendant enquiry as to where Irene was going. Irene had offered an explanation of sorts – a friend, an old friend, not someone Mother knew. Mother would be fine. She was sat in the kitchen with Ruth and Lily – a hub come suppertime now that Ruth had moved into the flat with her girls. The night times as jolly as coffee-time had been before, more so – much. The good bits of the day, the friendship parts were expanding, like the evenings, twilight starting to draw out. The dead weight of going-home time, once the darkest shadow of Irene's days, now seemed like some years-gone-by memory, some tinkling sound way out at sea.

'Spit 'em out then,' Nick The Builder said.

Irene raised an eyebrow. Sipped her glass of white wine. She hadn't even known what to ask for, he had suggested it. It was nice – made Irene think of lemons. And grass.

'Your demons,' Nick said. 'We're too long in the tooth not to start this thing off right.' Nick was a plain talker. 'Any particular reason you haven't married?' he asked. He had a pint of ale. He lifted it and drank, watching her over it.

'I had my mother,' Irene said, running her fingertip around the outside of her glass, making a line in the condensation. Then, liking his arrow approach and keen to warrant it, she said, 'And I didn't have any offers.'

He dipped his head, eyed her. 'You're aloof. Might put some men off.' His tone was pragmatic.

Not you, though, Irene thought, please not you. Maybe she was aloof. He seemed to know a lot about this sort of thing. More than her, not that that was much to say of anyone.

'What about you?' she asked.

'I was married,' he said. 'For twenty-four years. First five were pretty good and the last five were bad. The rest we were married. We're divorced now.'

'Children?'

'A daughter,' he said. 'Lives up north with her bloke.'

She nodded at this – parenthood, a world she could not comment on, like so many others. It made her feel…lacking in use.

Sensing something in her, discomfort, if not its source he said, 'When I said "long in the tooth", I didn't mean to say you were old. Just – not a kid. Not a silly kid, playing games. That's what I meant. I liked that about you first time I met you. That straightforward thing you have. I think the sex-appeal of efficiency is under-rated.'

'I'm forty-four,' Irene said. 'Forty-five in November. Beyond beauty, beyond babies. Beyond a lot of things.'

'Never say never.'

He was openly flirting with her. The great bright bawdy bubble of sexual promise was hanging between them. Of course Irene knew that if a man asked you out, as Nick had, brought you here to the Oyster Catcher for supper, as Nick had, and sat with you in a window table, wearing a decent shirt (shaved and showered after work)… If a man did those things, it might be more than friendship he had in his head. And yet she had not been sure. She had been searching all evening for tangible clues, because she was so unused to this sort of attention from a man, and she was, after all, in a way, Nick's employer. It was she who had confirmed that they would like him to refurbish the cottages, she who sorted out the budget and payments. She had told herself that he had asked her out as a Thank You. But this, this conversation was Date conversation. She, Irene, was on a Date. With Nick The Builder, who put his glass down now, and quickly, but not abruptly, lay his hand over hers on the table between them.

Irene kept her hand very, very still, the way a child who is an experienced lizard tracker does on spotting his target on a warm wall. She had felt nothing, other than distant, unrequited, adoration for men – as consistent and unpleasant as toothache – for as long as she could remember, now she was surprised by the twinkle of Looking Forward, of Fun, that she felt as the warmth of Nick's fingers – slightly calloused – seeped into her own

And then, in the car park.

He walked her to her car, opening the door, resting his hand again over hers on that thin strip above the window as if this were a long-established habit. She stood one side of it and he the other. He looked her in the eyes, his were brown as sugar on porridge.

'I know I said we're not kids,' he said. 'But I don't want you to think that I haven't noticed you've got a cute bum.'

Irene did not blush, but laughed. Across the road, beyond the sandy dip to the sea the sun was sinking. The sky was pink. Wasn't life grand? Wasn't life full of possibilities?

Lily, potting up lavender cuttings under the greenhouse's single bulb, 11:00 p.m., hears Irene's car arrive at Motthoe

and walks in the dark to the edge of the open garden area and sees Irene come to the blue door, silhouetted by the short-lived flood-lighting of the driveway behind. Irene is not looking for Lily and Lily knows it as soon as she sees her walk through the door and lean against the wall. Irene tips her head back and closes her eyes. This is detail unseen at Lily's distance. Still, Lily knows it. Irene is not in the garden looking for her, looking to unburden, but instead, like Lily, to drink it in. Irene stands straight again, steps down into the garden proper and picks a flower from the bush that Lily's cuttings have come from. She lifts it to her face and takes in the perfume. Then she walks back up to the house. She does not know that Lily is there, but she feels her presence, as a constant thing in that space. In her head she says goodnight to Lily. Her beautiful friend. And feels herself for the first time, inching over what once seemed an abyss between them – the abyss that divides the lovable from the not.

In that night moment in Lily's garden, Irene had been preserving her Perfect Evening, as best she could, remembering hard, in order to revisit it later, for the rest of her life maybe, as one of her most plainly joyful. Irene had not for a second guessed that it would lead to: her, Irene, in Nick's house, the following Saturday, in Nick's bed. Nick in the kitchen making breakfast.

Irene sat up and pulled the robe that Nick had lent her – paisley with green lining – from the seat of a small chair under the window. The chair had neat box pleats. She supposed that Nick's wife had decorated the house. It was very nice. Irene had always loved houses, loved the fantasy of them, the lives she imagined they sheltered and provided – it was what had first attracted her to working at Motthoe, though after the old man's death Harry had proved the glue. Then Motthoe and Harry had proved as disinterested in her ministrations as all life had been previously. Irene had accepted that; she had been so used to not getting what she longed for. So unquestioningly, habitually used to it.

Nick came back with the tray: eggs, smoked salmon, tea, wholemeal toast, white toast, jam. He put the tray in front of her.

'I see you had some provisions in,' Irene says, in her new bold persona.

Nick laughed. 'I could say that I was living in hope, but the truth is I generally live well.'

Irene was struck by this, she who had lived unwell for so very long, indulged not the slightest of her own whims. She had convinced herself until now that people who did were probably very selfish, unappealing. But here was Nick, neither of these. He sat in the bed near her, poured her tea and set it on the bedside cabinet.

'I like nice things and I like you,' he said.

Irene smiled, but for the first time felt nervous, distrustful. She had never seen that her skin was unlined, her chin pert and her eyes bright with intelligence. She had never seen that the wild kinks in her hair were lovely when not restrained and she had smiled too rarely to be aware of the effect. She took up her knife and fork and began on her eggs – decorated with chives. She had read those sorts of stories about silly women who got fleeced by flattering men. She thought about them now. Maybe it was worth the fleecing.

Nick said: 'After my wife left me, I was miserable. I saw much less of my daughter than I would have liked to. I went through a stage of making an idiot of myself with women. Women who I was bored by. I woke up in the mornings and wished them gone. I was looking for companionship, but also, I don't know…an ego-boost. I wanted confirmation that I was still manly, or whatever. Anyway, about eighteen months ago I jacked that in and took on a small building project. I have six young guys who work for me and I haven't been very hands-on in the business for the last few years, but I found that the work, especially renovating older properties, was really good for me. Did more for me than all the dolly-hunting. Got me back to myself.'

He had swung his legs up onto the bed, careful not to dislodge her tray, and stretched them out in front of him. They did not look at each other as he continued to speak. 'Then I met you, and there was something, I don't know, something so decent and frank about you. That's when I realized that women weren't the problem. It was just a question of meeting the right one. With a nice bum,' he said.

It was early still – Nick was a dawn riser, like her – as he put his hand to her face and cupped her chin, Irene hoped that her mother would sleep very late.

Mother asked Dan if she might hold the gun.

'It's heavy,' he said.   It was a twelve-bore. One of a pair of Purdeys that had once traveled England regularly in the company of Harry's great uncle, his father and an assortment of men like them. They had known charabancs, gartered socks, tweed waistcoats, and butler-served, sherry-laced bouillon, but now they saw only Motthoe's further reaches and Dan in his mud-caked boots.

'I can manage it,' she replied.

Dan looked at her and knew from the immense flat coolness of her returned stare that she could, that she had held a gun before. She had walked this far after all, startling him when he'd come across her, perched like an imp on a tree trunk at the edge of Cottle's Wood. Watching the birds, she'd said. She'd stood up and brushed the front of her skirt, a beige, pleated thing that reminded Dan of the librarians of his childhood.

'I can walk quite well,' she said, answering his thoughts, and gave him his first taste of that unswerving gaze. 'Although, for quite some time I forgot to,' she said. 'I think I lost interest in walking. The body is run by the mind you know, not vice versa.' She had set off then, lamb spry, towards the center of the field, and he with her, fearful for her thin ankles, visible below the skirt and above a pair of admittedly stout shoes.

'I'm eighty-eight,' she said. 'You need a pretty strong spur to get you going, a powerful scent. I lost wind of mine. Got stuck. That house with nobody but the neighbors and Irene to talk to. Nobody I liked.' She stopped dead and looked at Dan. 'You're shocked, I expect.'

Dan, too aware of his own failures to be shocked by those of others, answered her in the negative, but did so quietly, because, if he wasn't shocked, he did, nevertheless, feel something. Some waft of rapport with Irene.

'You're thinking of Irene,' the old lady said. 'I agree, it's appalling.' Then she set off again, with a smart intuition as to where to put her feet, sure in the grass hummocks and dips. 'I had her when I was forty-five,' she called back. Her voice, caught on a ruffle of breeze, turning reedy.

When Dan came beside her again, lengthening his own stride to do so, she repeated her statement.

'I had her when I was forty-five. Can you imagine?'

Dan could not.

'That was very old in 1962, far older than it is now. I had friends who were grandparents. It was an embarrassment. 'She'll be a blessing in your old age,' someone said to me once – as compensation, I suppose, for having to carry her about all those tiresome years when she was small. It wasn't as if there was any money either. Her father didn't care about that. Never one for practicalities. Didn't bother him that, just at the point when we should have been able to treat ourselves, we were tied to the house instead, spending money on school uniforms and bicycles. He adored her. Used to come in at night and look straight for her, walk right past me, calling out to her: "Where's Daddy's little tuppence then?" I was so jealous at times I might have harmed her. I never did, not in that way. Never physically. But then when her father died, well her grief somehow eclipsed my own and I thought, how bloody is that? How unfair, you barely knew him. She was eight.'

Dan had said nothing to all this, standing with the loaded shotgun broken over his forearm, staring over her head at the murk of the mid-morning sky. It had rained earlier. He thought of his own father. His own father who had shown him great affection, but in scant, inconsistent episodes. Episodes he had stopped relying on. He had his mother. His mother who cared for him and kept his room in her house in Oxford free in case he should want it. She was always there if he wanted her. At around fifteen he had started to think that he didn't, and now he didn't know. Strange bonds.

'And now of course, here she is, a blessing in my old age. I wonder if she'll ever know I realized that. May I…?'

He handed her the gun, barrel engaged. She raised it and hit a pigeon clean. 'There's a pie at least,' she said.

Dan, stunned, looked across her head to where the bird had fallen. She broke the gun. 'I'm glad I haven't forgotten,' she said. 'This is where I learned.'

'To shoot?'

'Yes, among other things.' She gave a light laugh, the sort of laugh that might have emanated from a much younger woman in different, more sumptuous surroundings. 'You had best say you shot it,' she said, turning to him and looking – within sight of the house – frail again. 'We don't want people fussing,' she said.

'No,' Dan agreed, they didn't. He fetched the bird and carried it back, with her walking ahead.

'Took herself for a walk,' Dan said to Ruth, laying the limp pigeon on the counter top, soft-necked, one painted eye to the saucepan rack.

'Good heavens,' said Ruth.

Irene's mother smiled like a child with a pocket full of stolen sweets.

Ruth settles her (all her puff gone after her adventures) in the kitchen armchair that is already as much hers as the garden is Lily's – domains being marked all over Motthoe. No harm has come of her outing, other than exhaustion and the attendant sluggishness of her wits.

Ruth takes advantage of the empty kitchen – still, but for the sleeping old woman – to cook, an activity in which she finds more and more assuaging satisfaction. She has shunned the nanny-flat's galley kitchenette for the main house's ample Victorian dimensions. She feels at home under the massive arch of the range-housing fireplace, admires the way that the beast-solid, staunch-legged chopping block holds its nerve under the lustiest grinding. They knew a thing or two about strength, about size in 1840, she thinks. She has enjoyed bringing the room back to what it should be; the center of something. She hangs the pigeon by his beak in the cool back larder; a task undertaken with great reverence for the creature that will provide a good supper, and in a pleasant haze of culinary puttering, she begins to bake.

It is the smell of hot sponge cakes to which Irene's mother wakes. She sits up, as Ruth transfers them from their tins to the wire rack, and begins to leaf through the fat recipe book that Ruth has set beside her.

'Shortbread,' she says. 'A great favorite of my husband's. You can substitute icing sugar, you know, for the other. It changes the texture – makes it very light.'

Ruth marveled at her recovered articulacy; at the way the brain apparently preserves itself in patches.

'But you don't really need advice, Ruth,' Irene's mother said. 'You have the touch.'

'I like baking,' Ruth said. 'Even more than other cooking. I liked making cakes and biscuits and whatnot when the girls were small. Flapjacks – they loved flapjacks – and cupcakes, they used to decorate them. That's what you do when they're small, isn't it? All those cake stalls and fêtes, you're forever baking – packed lunches. I missed it when they got older. They weren't interested then…sooner eat chocolate bars. Then the dieting set in. Now they don't want anything much I make, Ashley can still be tempted, but not Jess. Decides she's a vegetarian every six months, until she wants a bacon sarney. But I expect you had all that with Irene.'

'I don't remember,' the old lady said. 'I just liked baking.' She opened the recipe book again.

Ruth began to brush a batch of madeleines with sieved jam, watching the golden sheen come up on each cake. 'It's like brass polishing,' she said. 'Only without the elbow grease.'

'I hated housework,' the old lady said, closing the recipe book with crisp vehemence. 'Hated housework.'

Ruth paused, the pastry brush in her hand, the jam dribbling into the basin. 'I never minded it,' she said. 'Still don't. I like seeing the ironing all piled up finished and I like the smell of things when they're clean. And the order – I like things organized. Harder with the girls – I had to learn to close my eyes to their mess, put up with it. The clothes on the floor. All that.' She went back to the brushing, more slowly.

'I did it, of course,' Irene's mother said. 'I had no choice. And in my day women were much more judged on their ability to keep house. So, I did it, but it made me miserable. I think, if I had been born thirty years, forty years later I'd have been a slob. I think maybe it was the housework that turned me into such a bitch.'

Ruth stopped now and turned to her.

Irene's mother lowered herself back against her seat and smiled at Ruth, as if the word had freed her, freed something in her. For a moment she flitted there, her eyes up. Something on the ceiling had caught her attention.

Ruth finished the madeleines.

'It was all for nothing,' Irene's mother said, coming back. 'Most things are.'

Ruth, collecting the baking things, stacking them for washing, said, 'I think children are the point. I think children are what makes everything worthwhile. All my strength comes from my kids.'

'I was a terrible mother,' Irene's mother said. 'I knew it a long time ago. But I didn't know how to stop. I was fixed in my ways, you see, and there was no father. Irene's father died, so there was no father to tell me I was getting it wrong, or to make it up to her. I had her when I was forty-five. I wanted her to do well. I wanted her to do so well, so she could have the life I had wanted for myself, but I turned her weak, too weak to ever say no to me, too weak to ever answer back with a bit of spirit like that girl of yours does. I knocked all the spirit out of her. So, she stuck me, stuck me all her pathetic little life, all her spirit sucked out of her.'

She had delivered this speech to some mid-point, some absorbing space, in the kitchen that had grown silent with Ruth's listening. And each of her words had carried, so many clarion clangs, to Irene, standing, complexion still burnished from her lover's goodbye, at the rear, pantry door. She stood, in the aftermath of her mother's description of her, with a look on her face that was at first unreadable. Then it dissolved into pain. She turned without speaking and walked away.

After Irene's departure – as unseen as her arrival – her mother began to say something more: 'I wanted her to do well and I'm glad she's…I'm glad.'

Ruth went on with the clearing up. Until Irene came back again, as if for the first time. Composed. She took in the array of darling cakes.

'These are fantastic, Ruth,' she said.

'Your Mum's been giving me some tips,' Ruth said, wishing bridges could be built with compliments. Knowing they couldn't.

'Yes,' Irene said. 'She's always been good at baking.' A flat fact, no praise there.

Ruth, looking at her, wondered at the dire dynamic between the two of them. The mother who didn't want a child. The child who desperately needed a mother. A different sort of mother. None of it anybody's fault.

'She gets tired, though.'

'Yes,' Irene said, running a finger around the edge of the empty icing bowl and licking it.

'I wore her out, I think. She was a bit confused. This is her second nap.'

'Yes,' Irene said.

Ruth saw no point in mentioning the alarm of the surprise morning walk. 'Have you had a nice time?' she said.

Irene had only told her that she was visiting a friend – a school friend, she had hinted, but not exactly said. Vague as Harry.

Irene paused from licking the spoon. 'I have,' she said, and the tsunami comprehension of the truth of this washed all her mother's failings away.

CHAPTER SEVEN

H arry noticed that Irene was different. For one thing she had stopped making coffee. Harry didn't mind that Irene had stopped making coffee, he had never asked her to in the first place. But she had definitely stopped. She had stopped looking at him as if bluebirds were circling his head, too. This was disconcerting, although he had not particularly enjoyed it at the time. She had changed. And now this.

She confronted him with a pile of accounts. Set them up on his desk. Invoices and ledgers and cheque books and printout statements from banks and credit cards. And then she gave the top of the pile a snappish click with a sharp pencil when she instructed him to take a look.

'These are my notes,' she said, finalizing the switch from schoolgirl to school marm.

It was perplexing, sudden change like that, especially in a woman. Harry did not feel that he had ever really understood women. He knew that there were a lot of men of his generation who did understand them. He knew that his attitudes, honed in single-sex schooling and a lack of female relatives in his teens, were outmoded. But he had realized too, since coming back to Motthoe that a great deal of him was as old fashioned as his surroundings. As old fashioned as his father had been. How was it possible to be so much like someone from whom you had been so soundly estranged?

Harry pulled his chair closer to his desk and ignoring Irene's Pile of Practicalities for the moment, lifted an envelope that he had come across earlier that day and slid a sheet of off-white Basildon Bond from its interior. Why had he kept the letter? He was just someone who kept things. Like his father.

Harry, the letter began, *you are my son and your mother's son and it is on account of the latter that I continue to have some expectations of you, though you have proved unworthy of them so far. It is my heartfelt prayer, and has been always, that, for the sake of her memory, if not for my approval, which I have come to realize means little to you, you will attempt to make something of yourself.*

I hoped for many years that you would return to Motthoe and learn its ways, learn how to make your place here. I could do with some assistance; the running of the estate is not, as you know (or can at least imagine, after your long absence) the same job it was even in my father's time. It requires a much more hands-on approach now. I have spent today, in fact, assisting with some much-needed roof repairs – work that you, as a younger and fitter man, might have undertaken were you here. Still, enough of that, you are not.

I mention these things now – things upon which I would prefer not to dwell, or remind myself of at all – only because Doctor Hislop has told me today that my emphysema will get the better of me sooner rather than later. I tell you this, Harry, not for sympathy, but to impress upon you that the running of Motthoe will be your responsibility, your duty, before long. I am urging you one final time to take that fact on board and to make some serious attempt to educate yourself re the requirements.

Harry imagined his father writing these words. It wasn't difficult. He could see the man, barely bent over his study desk, shoulders back, his tweeded elbow crooked just so, the look of subdued, but discernible disappointment held back by his strict belief (and teaching) that all negativity sat perilously atop the skiddy slope to despair and its attendant evils. Harry knew that this image was a caricature, but he was only ever able to draw his father in these thick outlines. He attempted to meld the picture with the one that Irene's mother had painted – the brave, admired, humanitarian boy. He couldn't do it. He decided that the boy had been blotted out long before he had known the man.

Harry set his father's written appeal next to an empty tea mug advertising farming equipment aware that Irene had just made the same appeal, if less indirectly (and she had not removed the tea mug, as she might have once).

'Harry,' she'd said, 'these are the books for the last six months. I will discuss them with you in the morning once you have had a chance to study them.' Her new confident eyes had insisted: educate yourself re the requirements. Get a grip, Harry.

Harry lifted the notes and began to read them – even Irene's handwriting seemed to have taken on authority.

First, Irene had written, take a look at the balances, then at the areas I have marked where I think expenditure could be reduced. Any input you have would be useful.

Useful input, thought Harry. There's a challenge.

Harry decides that his latest project – a bat house – is the wrong project; the bats are happy roosting in the beams of the many, derelict unvisited outbuildings that Motthoe offers them. The bat house had not started out as a bat house, but a second attempt at an owl house. Harry had recently stood and watched a tawny owl, settled on a fence post as still as if he was an extension of it – shimmery in late afternoon light. The owl had sat there like some mythical thing, letting Harry be a part of its unreal existence for a moment, a long enough moment for Harry to forget his lack of natural aptitude with a hammer.

Once, when he was a child, a large white barn owl had come to live above the back stables and hatched her offspring there. Harry's father had taken him to see it. Harry must have been very small because outings with his father like that became rare after he reached the age of speaking back, but he remembered it for two things: one, that his father had lifted him, the feel of his jacket, bristly on the back of Harry's legs. And two: that just as he had, welding these events for ever, the owl had flown out and over them, low and clean over their heads. Harry had cried out and buried his head. His father, whipping round to watch the owl, had said, 'Marvelous, bloody marvelous, Harry. Look.' As the owl had skimmed the land and disappeared over the back of the house. Harry had not been scolded for his fear. Perhaps his father had not noticed, or perhaps, despite the exactness of the memory, he had been very small indeed.

That was why he had thought to put the owl houses up in the first place. He had headed for the handyman's superstore on the outskirts of town – a twenty-nine-mile round trip – with a song in his heart and a buoyant feeling of being just another guy with a credit card and a list. At the store, navigating the aisles – so clean and orderly, indistinct music playing in the background – feeling excited, almost elated that so much of this stuff existed: flammable stuff, stuff that proclaimed in unsloping, no-nonsense black lettering that it was for Outdoor Use Only. Harry had felt that maybe, after all, there was a lot he could do himself at Motthoe – not everything, obviously, but the smaller things. Things that had just been let go. He had filled his cart with pre-sawn lumber, and cans and tools. Ready.

At the checkout, pleased with himself, he unloaded the results of his good humor on to the counter and attempted to make light conversation about his potential projects with the teenaged boy who was manning it. The response – animated as tarmac – was his first taste of the disappointment that would follow. Later, he had started on the owl houses; it was the day that Lily had come, and if it hadn't been for her arrival it would have sunk into unmitigated hopelessness even more muddily than it had.

Dan had laughed at the owl plan, all along: the owls were as well catered for as the bats and rats at Motthoe, he had said, and Harry needed to focus on the main building. Harry had known Dan was right, but at the time it had been small consolation. He had shoved the tools and the other doings – mostly still packaged – in a back-room cupboard because looking at them made him feel ashamed. He had spent money unnecessarily, and he had failed again to produce anything worthwhile. He was still the boy with his head buried in his father's coat, missing the sight of anything majestic.

And yet today, today he had determined to try again.

The new project Harry sets himself: a troublesome lavatory on the second floor. It isn't an ancient lavatory, not like the one downstairs at the side of the mudroom with its mighty overhead flush and Victorian fixings, but a shabby 1996 affair – plastic seat and fixings in a flabby sort of peach. Nevertheless, it is Harry's bathroom lavatory and it is not working, which necessitates a cold sally down a chilly corridor for Harry most mornings at 6:00 am. Harry finds this an inconvenience.

Today, calmly, he lifted the lid from the cistern and could see, just as suggested by the illustration on the instructions he'd looked up, that the chain link, flimsy and fake looking, has indeed broken free from the hook that operates the flush mechanism. He lowered his hand to it through the water in the cavity, his hand feeling fat and blundering in the space, and the chain, slippery, dropped from his fingers on the first two attempts. But eventually, he was able to lift it and loop it again over the hook.

That was it. It worked.

Harry waited till the water refilled and tugged the handle again. He had fixed it. He put the lid back on the cistern, washed and dried his hands and looked at himself in the mirror. He had fixed something. He is a hero.

Dan writes: 6 x 8" bamboo. Twine – runner bean frames – in his journal, which has thickened of late. He has new interests. Since Lily's arrival, and the expansion of the Motthoe populace, he has begun to grow a few vegetables. Lettuces first – dug in two rows in a patch of well-draining soil on the upside of one of Lily's walls. He's been rewarded by their quick flourishing. He has enjoyed carrying the soft new leaves up to the kitchen, lingering there while Ruth rinses them and shakes them to dry. Now he's put in some radishes. Ogden, who had kept a good vegetable patch while his wife was alive to cook them, has shown him how to grow potatoes in sand and told him about bean frames.

Dan has written about the vegetables; what is growing, what is taking, what needs water, feed and yields, what has been made from them and who has eaten it, in the journal he'd once kept for fiction. It is the first writing he has ever done that has a joyful aspect, though he is unaware of this, seeing for now only practicality, not the pleasure that has begun to seep through.

He asked Lily for some advice on compost.

She put her fork down and righted herself from her spot at the border edge. The soil there was damp and she'd kneeled on a grain sack to tend to the fine weeding, turning carefully, avoiding the delicate roots of verbena and lobelia. She looked at him: she the diligent missionary, he the child who asks about Jesus.

She followed him up and looked over his little growings. She could have done so before, she had heard his work, twinning hers on the other side of the wall, and had eaten the lettuces, but made no comment until one was sought. Now she showed him how to heap his soil, how to plant in triangles, how to secure vines so that they would not tear off in wind. She tapped her chin and left him and came back with nasturtium seeds to till amongst his crops.

The next day they had gone to market together, she with potted cuttings, and tied flower bunches: daisies and tulips. They had brought back asparagus and seed potatoes.

Driving back, eyes ahead, the smell of peat between them, Dan said, 'I'm beginning to understand the appeal of gardening.'

'Yes,' Lily said.

Dan glanced at her, in his car, just a little out of place – her flowing hands stilled in her lap in the passenger seat.

'There's something almost addictive about it,' he said. 'You start off with a few lettuces, and then you're… drawn in. Considering artichokes.'

She laughed and Dan wanted to get a hook into that commitment.

'It's the flowers for you, isn't it?' he said.

Lily thought about it. 'Flower gardening is a bit like painting with very thin paint – paint that will fade, or wash away,' she said. 'So, you have to make the painting as splendid as you can for the short time that it will be seen. If you grow flowers, you're looking all the time for the moment…when everything is perfect. When everything is at its best. It doesn't happen very often. Sometimes, even if it does, it only lasts for a few hours. Sometimes, most times, I am not there when it happens. But I like to feel I had a part in it.'

Later he wrote down what she had said. They were becoming friends and that made him more sensitive to the thing in her that was kept apart. He thought about the night when he'd seen her take up the broom, lift it as a weapon against Ogden. The way she had stood there, long after he had gone, long after threat was over. He supposed that a girl who was a nomad like that, moving from place to place would be naturally wary, but he suspected it had been more than that.

Dan went back to his list. He had overwatered the courgettes – Ogden had told him so – he needed to check on them. Ogden had also said that there were bees at the farm; the hive a bit neglected and they wanted some tending in the winter, perhaps they could move the hive up here. Maybe extend the bee-keeping if Dan thought he'd like to learn it. Dan thought he would. Bees, beans: new, new life.

Lily wrote: *Blondine* on the last page of notebook # 57 and pressed the creamy tulip petal to her lips. She had established that it was *Blondine* by searching Harry's mother's entries in the Motthoe logs. *Blondine*, Dutch, rare, tall and elegant as Harry's mother had been. Perhaps it was in deference to her that Lily set the completed notebook on a shelf, rather than on the littered bench of the greenhouse. She set it up and away, like something to be cherished.

Today she had removed two, blobby masses of fuchsias, which she guessed anyway to have been hasty gap-fills, unrelated to the true body of the garden, and replaced them with phlox. And then, standing back, wiping her hands she saw the combination of these efforts, and those that had gone before, and before that – the hands that had guided hers – and saw that the garden was on the verge of celestial. It was dotted with nodding fritillaries – plum-colored elves' hats – lace hydrangea heads and chiffon ranunculus. Lily's eyes ran along a swathe of rusty rudbeckia. She wondered if Harry's mother would mind that she had added cottage flowers in the holes that the digging out had left and decided that no one who had ever loved anything could object to Sweet William.

Beyond the garden, nature was competing with Lily's handiwork – wild garlic and red campion, carpeting purslane – and behind her the sun made infernos of Motthoe's window panes. She wanted to be forever in a beautiful place like this, beautiful places made her feel peaceful inside, safe almost. She could not have explained it, but she knew it to be true nevertheless. Ugliness: grim tarmac, mean buildings, gray pylons and nasty, thoughtless pedestrian planting, bunchy chrysanthemums struggling for life beneath balled up supermarket bags – the sorts of things she had lived with, in the sorts of places she had grown up in, depressed her, and worse, made her anxious. As crowds did – in crowds the face one wants to forget, which one can banish almost entirely from mind in waking hours, has a tendency to appear without warning on the bodies of strangers.

In her early vagabond years when distance had seemed paramount, Lily had traveled north, but she had found the winters there too hard on her trade, the seasons too short, so she had come south west again, and found enough prettiness to sustain her. But, in every other garden Lily had tended, she had only felt divided from the discords of life outside, by a fence, or a road or two, a few miles of lanes separating village from town. At Motthoe she felt as if they had vanished completely. In Lily's Garden, she felt as if nothing could ever harm her, as if this were the whole, heavenly world. She felt sometimes, and the thought amazed her, that she would like to stay there for ever. But she could not.

Lily followed the length of the curving pathway to the hedge gap, recently reopened, in the eastern corner. She had asked Ogden to repair a wooden bench to put behind there. Now she sat on it. Beside her, early white roses spread over mottled red brick. The sun fell in slants across the paving. She closed her eyes and let the songs of the birds fill her head.

Harry took a three-branched, French ormolu candelabra from a shelf in the room that had been referred to in his father's childhood as the silver room. There was silver there still, but nobody had referred to it much at all for twenty or so years.

The shelves had been relined in one of Ruth's gallant attempts to hold Motthoe together, but the plasterwork had come away in lumps. Harry put the candelabra down and picked out a silver platter from a stack of three (once thirty) and shook it so that lumps of wall and ceiling fell from it onto the floor. He took the candelabra and the tray with him, dragging the door open with his foot and kicking it closed again.

In the dining room Harry's forebears watched from the walls, some disapproval among them, as he set the candelabra in the center of the George III mahogany dining table that had been bought to replace the magnificent Pollard oak version that had sat there for a hundred years – sold in 1990, the profits gone into bathroom renovations and sundry roofing. He set the tray down on a bow-fronted sideboard and took from it a canteen of engraved silverware – mostly intact. He would ask Ruth to polish it. Two auctions in his father's time and one in his, and yet these things remained. These things which, he supposed, nobody else had any use for. He had supposed this after the last auction, when several items which he had imagined a great many people would have a use for had failed to meet their reserves. The chap from the auction house – impeccable of attire and expression – had refrained from lapsing into even the vaguest of I-told-you-so smirks. Nevertheless, he had managed to tell Harry so. Harry, for all his denseness in many areas (Women, for example. Getting down to things, for another), could detect under-mutterings. It was a skill he was born to.

The dining room felt cool and Harry opened a window, guessing correctly that the outdoor air was warmer. He imagined his Uncle Henry frowning in his frame behind him.

Uncle Henry, older than Harry's grandfather, a great uncle in fact, represented one of the sideways skips in Motthoe's passage through the family line. In the late eighteenth century the estate had been in the hands of the Lewins, it had fallen to a family named Hendon after that, and in 1937 uncle Henry – a nephew of Clarissa Hendon, whose pale image as a nineteen-year-old debutante still graced a guest bedroom – had inherited. Henry had known Motthoe in the days when a boy was always on hand with a soda siphon and he had remained to the end willfully ignorant of the fact that, by 1949, Motthoe was run by a live-in housekeeper and a handful of part-timers from the village. Henry had sat on more than one occasion beneath a dead light bulb, waiting for the appropriate employee to come and change it. He died, wifeless, daughterless, sonless and friendless, of a massive coronary in 1951, saving everyone a lot of trouble. It thus that the house had come for a short time to Harry's grandfather, then to Harry's father, and then to him. Harry could still feel these generations at his back – the push of them. He turned and looked at the portraits for a moment and let their collective expectations wallop him full on.

'But I am here,' he said to them. 'I am the one who is here.'

Harry was more Here, in fact, than he had ever been. As a child he had never really lived at Motthoe, not that he could remember. After his mother's death he had lived variously with his maternal grandmother (whose pretty Tudor cottage, which had come to him on her death, he had sold in order to invest in a spectacularly ill-advised restaurant project), and under the care of nannies, one of whom took him home with her for three months, to no objection from his father. Then school, from seven, and holidays with friends. Until he had come back.

During those first months as castellan, the great vast loneliness and melancholy of Motthoe had overwhelmed Harry, driven him to take up camping in two rooms in the west wing. At night he had watched his television there, alone, and tried to imagine that his life was straight forward, free from albatrosses. When he did see other people – walking their dogs, buying their bread, kissing their wives goodbye on doorsteps – he imagined, as everyone who is lonely in their troubles does, that the problems faced by such people were of the straightforward, explainable type – fitted to straightforward, explainable solutions. It was a low spell.

Harry wants everyone to sit in the dining room and eat together. A Beginning, though as yet the future pattern is not clear in his head or theirs. They don't know, that first night, that if they are not in Lily's garden come the evening-time this summer, they will be here. All of them: Harry, Dan, Ruth and Jess and Ashley, Lily, Ogden, Irene and often Irene's mother. And then, to come, young Jason and Irene's Nick, but not yet. They would be there, with all the windows open, looking out, looking at each other, smiling, talking. Slowly they'd begin to dress up, to dress for the silver. Flowers in Lily's hair. All of them pooling resources. Ogden up with a haunch of venison. Ruth showing Irene how to marinate it. Make a red wine sauce. Dan digging and Lily peeling the potatoes. Delicious. Evenings to come. And others, less welcome.

For now, here they are that first night. Quaint, and curious, too, the way they file in to dinner in neat procession, just as they might have done in Harry's Mother's day. Perhaps it is the surroundings, the room, that quiets them, brings out a subdued formality. Dan and Harry, old habits, held chairs for the women.

And now, as everyone sits – Harry, Lord at his table, in his father's place – a current runs through them – the tiny, infectious thrill of differentness. Harry takes on the authority of his head-of-table chair, and when Jess comes in with the salmon (Harry has offered her and Ashley a tenner apiece to wait on them) and heads for him first, he indicates with a gentle, but kingly nod that she should serve Irene's mother first, seated on his right. And Jess does, while Ashley takes her cue from this and begins to pass out the plates in the other direction, 'Lean in from the left', mimes Harry. As the servings made their way along the table toward Lily, who was sat at the opposite end, facing him, Harry turns to Ruth and asks her how she is finding living in Nanny's Flat. Just as if, Ruth thinks, just as if she had not been in this room that very morning, polishing in her pinny.

In fact, the look Harry gives Ruth, and his manner, the tone of his voice, makes her feel as if she is, exactly, someone new to his acquaintance, a woman, a lady. It makes Ruth feel quite tearful, and almost slim.

Dan, to Lily's left, similarly transformed, strikes up an almost-charming gambit with Irene, and beside her, Mother smiles the smile, if not of the joyful, at least of the content.

During dinner a good, raisiny Riesling was offered, but Lily refused it. She was doing these small things for her baby.

Nevertheless, most of the time, the chrysalis inside her had flourished without acknowledgement since her first fleeting acceptance of its existence. Lily, product herself of a tough raising, if diligently resistant to its ravages, understands that it is not pregnancy that she has to come to terms with, nor even a baby – strung prettily asleep in a scarf hammock at her breast – but a child. And, one day, a grown girl, like Jess and Ashley, and what comes with that – culpability, restraint. Lily is afraid. How will she, Lily, van driver and nomad, help a child with her homework, teach a child to cook, give a child a home – the way that Ruth is doing? The way that Lily's mother did not. Lily, taking the divergent way that every unhappy child treads, had vowed to do the exact opposite to her own parent and never to treat a child as a portable charm, a plaything for the few moments such a thing was wanted. Lily had made not only the easy, bedrock pledges – she would never hit a child, or neglect it – but the more slippery ones, too: she would never hug a child to suffocation, never frighten her with her own leaking need. 'My little love, Lil. My precious darlin', my princess. My reason for living.' All sensation, all emotion. It had worn off on Lily by the time she was nine.

How could she have a baby? She could not. How could she not have this one? She could not. And so, Lily has tight-roped these past weeks above the mire of her concerns, twirling her fantasy parasol. But tonight, the butterfly turns bird. Lily knows that the sensations she has been vaguely aware of until now are not true movement, merely some trick of physiognomy, internal rearrangement – possible to ignore. Now she clutches the table edge, the white cloth smooth and starched beneath her fingers, as the undeniable push of something, of life, presses outwards from her abdomen.

Lily excuses herself early from the evening and is drawn to her greenhouse like a salmon upstream, refuses offers of company. Leaving, looking back into the room she sees the lights in the eyes and the loveliness of the scene, but notes that without her contributed anemones – spilling from three engraved christening cups – the picture would be lacking.

In the loamy greenhouse quiet, she distracts herself by tweaking out some plugs – minute fragile roots. The compost has been warming all day and she beds the roots gently in their growing-on pots, tucked in all around, strokes their nascent sprigs with caressing fingers. She blows Lily breath on them. Goodnight.

She walks the field to Ashcott more slowly than usual, the path at the hedge-line well-worn now from her crossings. Irene has given her a torch, but on good moon nights like tonight she does not need it. A shrew darting across her path does not startle her. Her feet take her to her makeshift, mobile vehicle bed like faithful ponies.

In the morning, when she rises from her tossing sleep, lately more uncomfortable in the back of her van, she pushes its rear doors open and turning to seal them again, to go into the cottage for tea as is her habit, she finds a hat; a baby's hat, like the top of an acorn, like something an elf would wear, hanging on the wing mirror.

Lily lifted the hat down and put her hand inside it. It seemed warm, almost as if recently worn, by a real baby. Lily guessed that Ruth had put it there – as a sign for her.

A sign that she could talk when she wanted to. She didn't want to. Not yet. But talk or no, there was a rent in her cover, there would be no ducking the facts of her future now. Not while she lived at Motthoe. The Departure Clock tick had struck up.

Distraction is the friend of feet (and hearts and minds) that are about to tackle a heavy climb, so when Lily's walk to the garden that morning intercepted Harry's, she agreed to join him and they made their way together, but under Harry's lead, into the woods and along a wide track – wide enough for two people to walk side by side without feeling confined. Lily began to enjoy the walk. Harry was already enjoying it more.

'I prefer the woods to the more open spaces,' he said.

Lily felt a kinship with him here. 'I like the way they let the sun in,' she said. 'Just when you least expect it.'

'Yes,' Harry said. 'There is something special about the unexpected.'

Lily was not so sure about this in general terms, but she inferred its undertone. 'The expected is a burden to you sometimes, isn't it, Harry?'

'I don't think I consider myself burdened. I hope not, in fact. I have a responsibility is more how I see it.' He swung his stick, keeping his eyes straight ahead. 'It's as if a part of history has been passed to me, like an egg on a spoon. And if I dropped it, I would be – not me somehow. It's hard to...'

'I see,' Lily said. She stooped to pick up a piece of elder. She toyed with it, walking evenly, waiting. The sun dipped in and out behind the clouds, behind the trees, the air smelled damp and slightly fungusy. Their feet crunched on dried leaves beneath them.

'It's just a thing – in my life. You are aware of it, yet not aware of it at the same time, like being tall,' Harry said.

Like being pregnant, thought Lily. 'Yes,' she says to Harry.

The track ended in a semi-circle. There were tyre marks in the mud, a vehicle had turned here since it last rained; Forestry people, Harry said. Traces of life even in somewhere that felt so untouched. That was England, populated from top to bottom. It was a wonder there was anywhere like this at all. Lily was grateful that there still was. Harry's onus, she thought, was an oasis to her.

'Do you want to go down to the brook?' Harry asked, already heading to the narrower downward path through the trees.

'Yes,' she said. It wasn't far. The path dipped only slightly and not sharply, though it was boggy in places, being all the way shaded over.

'Watch your step,' Harry called.

Lily was glad she had walked with him, not just for the pleasure of the foxgloves, but because she had discovered he had something of the plantsman in him. Harry, it seemed, had no memory of the garden as anything but choked and overgrown, although he must have known it in previous tended times – it was, thought Lily, as if the unhappiness inside a person filtered their view of the outside like shaded eye glasses. But despite his neglect of the borders and his ignorance of the plants they contained, he had, a few moments before, pointed out several young elms to her, with a look close to passion.

'It's important to encourage them, obviously,' he said, and seeing from her expression that it was his turn to educate, he had explained what elm disease had done to the woods. 'Nobody agrees now on what sorts of elms they've got, but it doesn't matter. It is just so good to see something reviving.'

'Yes,' said Lily again.

They had reached a clearing next to the brook – rumbly sounding from recent rain. He picked up a dead wood scrap and threw it, as if the end of the walking had left him with nothing to do – a vacuum in which he was floundering.

Lily leaned against a tree trunk and lifted her face up to the sky.

'There's a swimming hole further up where it widens,' Harry said. He pointed. 'Half a mile, or so that way. There's a track, or was, I expect it's grown over by now. You'd have to wade. Perhaps if the weather gets warm again.'

'Yes,' she said, and looked at him.

He, bumbly from direct contact, began to poke at the lower vegetation at the edges of the clearing. A kingfisher darted over the water.

Lily sank down the tree trunk, sat and closed her eyes and Harry walked a little into the water. He crossed and stood for a moment on the opposite bank and played his stick at the ground. 'Who the hell does that?' he thought, coming across a cigarette butt, burying it the soft earth. 'Someone who doesn't belong here.'

Rob, Ruth's erstwhile husband, stubbed out his cigarette in a brown pottery ashtray and lowered his head to his hands. He had not known before Ruth and the girls had left that a silent house could engender physical pain. But it had. The loss had been like something ripped out – left gaping. He wanted to tell her that. He wanted to tell her right now, to hitch a lift to that place she was living in, and stand in front of his wife of twenty years, the girl he'd loved since they'd messed around flirting with each other over lukewarm cider at the May Day fête – him eighteen, her sixteen. He wanted to say, 'Look, Ruth. I've fixed it. I'm off the booze and I've got a job. Come back, Ruth. I miss the girls, I love you.' But only the last seven words would be true. He looked at the card in his left hand, turned it over. He read the card again: Alcoholics Anonymous. Meetings in the hall behind the Methodist church in Allan Street. He stood up and put the card in his back pocket.

CHAPTER EIGHT

Summer; Irene is in love. Ruth knows it. Lily knows it. The Motthoe air is so lush with this fact that everybody knows it, whether they know they know it, or not. Irene sings – flutey tunes, half-hummed, trail her in the passages. She puffs her mother's pillows with gladsome geniality. She holds herself differently, is lighter in her stance, in her everything. She reaches for tea cups with a loose, adolescent swing. She loves Nick, and as the days stretch on, she steadies in her knowledge of his love for her. He's as reliable as the tide, as kind as a warm bath. And he has set desire murmuring, fizzing inside her like Epsom salts.

In the kitchen, in Lily's garden – and with Lily and Ruth only – Irene starts to say 'Nick'. Testing at first; just the word, just the breathing of it causing her cheeks to heat, but she gets over that and can drop him in now whenever she likes, straightforward as tossing pebbles – Nick this, Nick that, because Lily and Ruth don't tease. There is no giggling, nothing unseemly or prying when Ruth says: 'You'll be wanting some more help with your mother, so you can spend more time with your man.' *Your Man.*

And Lily says: 'Nice solid name, Nick. Like "Oak".'

There it was. Done. He is there, in their conversation, telephoning her, sending his protecting care through the ether to her, all the time. But she has not brought him in person yet to Motthoe. She will. She would, if it weren't for Mother. Lately, Mother is kinder, less likely to carp, or bite. This morning she has said 'moon' when she meant 'noon' and Irene has asked, unthinkingly (ordering scent bottles on the dresser) for clarification, 'Do you mean "noon", Mother?' Then her hand, as if the realization came upwards from here to her head, had paused above a bisque figurine of a little girl – loved by Harry's mother, unnoticed by hers – while she waited for the sting of reprimand.

None had come. Irene's mother, turning toward her had merely repeated 'Moon, noon, moon...' and smiled. Irene had smiled back. Nevertheless, forty-four years don't wipe off completely clean.

'I'll remember,' says Lily. 'I'm used to doctoring things.'

Irene, who has seen Lily measuring liquid feed with a plastic bottle cap, dripless, into a full watering can, believes her, but continues to check her mother's pills off in her new, unhurried manner. This will be Lily's first time with sole responsibility for Mother. Ruth will be at the school this evening (Parents' Night. She will drive there with a rock in her stomach.)

Lily says Irene is to spend her evening with Nick and enjoy it, not to worry. She can manage.

'This one helps her to sleep. There's linctus here for her chest if the cough is dry. These are for her joint pain...'

Lily puts a hand on Irene's arm: 'Love suits you, Irene,' she says.

And Irene begins, quietly, silently to weep. In her hand a packet of tin-foiled tablets shakes. Who knew? she thinks. Who knew there was Happy like this, in the stars, for me?

Lily smiles, pulls a tissue from the box at Mother's bedside. Enjoy your evening, she says. And Irene sniffs and blows her nose and thanks Lily and goes off to see why Harry is bellowing for her up the stairs. Lily stays to reorder the pill bottles, lining them up like soldiers, before she leaves.

Lily has not been above the ground floor at Motthoe before. She has never had occasion to mount the wide expanse of the front staircase, or take the steep, ill-lit climbs of the rear ones. She knows the kitchen, and the front, the dining and Harry's sitting room. But this, the upper expanse of the house – the floors that offer intimacy with their history – were new to her. On her way down, she lingered at the end of a short gallery and stood at the window with the rickety curtain where the lamenting Harry had stood on that early day, a long time ago, watching her with Irene, and she saw a hawk circle above a cornfield on the east edge of the woods.

The hawk circled and Lily, though she did not want to watch it, was caught, hypnotized by its slow round and round in the hard blue sky. Round and round it went, the circles tightening, and Lily's heart quickened. She stood, looking out of that window – Georgian, extending above her head, a narrow sill at knee height, an exposing window – mesmerized by the hunter's lazy, focussed cruise. It had prey on its mind and all the time in the world to catch it. Lily stared. Her heart was firing as quick and hard as the heart of the mouse, or shrew, or whatever small thing was scurrying in the corn. The sun was still commanding bright. The hawk dipped and swayed. All else was still. Except the mouse, Lily thought. Was the mouse, occupied with its mouse life, aware of the hawk? Was it racing now for shelter, for protection, or was it playing, oblivious to the wing-shaped shadow that would blot out the light – the hawk too large, too far off to be recognizable as foe?

The hawk dived and rose with the creature in its beak. Lily imagined she saw the thing struggle, heard its final squeal. She knew she did not. The screams she heard were inside her own head – where she had always kept them. She turned from the window. It was over at least. The mouse was dead, it did not have to feel its terror over and over. Did not have to keep running. Lily had thought, more than once in her life that being dead was probably a lot better than being terrified.

Irene thought that she might never feel fear again. Not in the clammy-palmed way she had felt it before; fear of judgement. But new feelings were filling this absence. She put a hand to her hair. Lily had told her to grow it and to stop blow-drying it, had given her the rosemary shampoo. And now here she was, Irene, with sleek curls, waves where the frizz had been, feeling strangely sad. There had been an answer all the time. A simple answer to a life-long vexation. So many days wasted in the draining grip of minor upset.

'You look great,' Nick said.

It is not just the hair. It is the lack of worry about her mother. About not having to get up in the night. And also, this, Nick. Nick's bed. It has changed everything. Up at Motthoe this morning her mother will sit in the kitchen, while Ruth breaks eggs, slices bread. Benign domesticity. While here, just him and her. Nick and Irene. So far, so many steps into exotic paradise.

Jason, the Grass Lad, has volunteered to come up Sundays to help in the garden – spurred by the sproutings there like everyone else. Ruth, fetching out bacon sandwiches for anyone who wants them, says hello to the boy and then, mind rolling, thinks…maybe Jess…(who is on the grass now squabbling with Ashley and shaking her hair – two weeks till end of term, already restless, eyelashes caked with contraband mascara – Ruth has decided to save this battle for the time being), maybe Jess, thinks Ruth, and Young Jason – quiet, hardworking, son of a doctor. Not much of a smiler, but decent, working for free, helps out – bright kid with the right values.

'Ooh,' she says, putting down the meat carving dish on which she has piled the sandwiches and paper napkins. 'Here's Jason. Have you met Jason, Jess? Ashley?'

'Nope,' says Ashley. Cuffs her sister, sets off another round of pandemonium.

Jess barely looks at Jason. From over the wall, and the fields and the trees they hear the bell from the village church as it rings in the start of service – once, twice, three times.

Ruth gives up and sets about making a chair sturdy enough for Irene's mother. Irene's mother is called Edith, but everybody still calls her Irene's mother. As if we were connected, Irene sometimes thinks, by chain-link. But, of course, they are not, because Irene is only just now turning in to the driveway and hoping that no one will see her do so, hoping that eyeballs won't glide in her direction, hoping that several sets of lips will not tic subtly, simultaneously, with collective knowingness. Irene knows her hankering for an unmarked arrival is unrealistic, but old habits – unrealistic hankerings in Irene's case – die tough. She parks by the old stable block and hides there, like a prowler.

Lily is showing Jason the potting-up she has in mind for him – strong thumbs, she figures him for, and that's what she needs, no namby-pambying, wants someone to thumb the compost around the roots nice and solid. She does not realize that as she stands talking to him her hand goes to that small part of her back that a pregnant woman always finds.

And then it travels in a tell-tale caress across her lower belly.

Irene having stood her moment in the shade of the house, breathing out, breathing in, affects a strolling gait to the garden where she keeps her eyes down while giving her Good Mornings and engaging herself swiftly in aiding the nestling of Mother, who is in fact quite nimble, her knees seeming less troublesome since their move to Motthoe along with everything else about her. She seems at times now, Irene thinks, draping her lap with the car rug that Ruth has followed brought – over her arm like a sommelier's cloth – almost the Grande Dame; gracious, as if she were mistress of Motthoe, of all she surveyed. She does not remark on Irene's night-long absence. But does, just as Irene stands – having over-patted the blanket into its place, tucked it too diligently at the sides, double-, triple-checked the balance of the chair – catch her with a look that suggests she is aware of it. Irene, a grown woman, almost squirms.

'The flowers in your room must be going over,' says Lily, approaching on light feet, honeying the moment. 'There's plenty in bloom at the back and it's still shady there if you fancy some picking.' She hands Irene a pair of scissors and a mason jug with water. 'Put them straight into the water,' she says. 'It keeps them fresh.'

This last word, in Lily's accent, from Lily's mouth drips more than any lascivious look. Irene takes up the scissors and jar and scarpers for the far borders.

'I had her when I was forty-five,' Irene's mother says, just as a dense bank of slate cloud scuds over the woods and obscures the sun. Everyone in the garden is silenced for a moment, looking up at it, wondering if the dry morning will hold. 'Can you imagine?'

Ruth turned to the old lady, though she was still watching her daughter, at the end of the garden now, almost out of sight, out of hearing certainly, out of scrutiny, she hoped. '"She'll be a blessing in your old age," someone said to me once. I had to carry her about all those tiresome years, you know, when she was small. It wasn't as if there was any money either – in the war. Nobody had any money,' she said.

'The war?' Ruth said.

'Yes, my dear,' Irene's mother replied, all at once Duchess-voiced. 'It made us all thrifty – thrifty and dutiful.'

Ruth, confused, knowing that Irene had been born well after the war, decided not to pursue the matter. She had corrected Irene's mother, mildly, on some event's timing once before, and received a quick telling-off for her trouble. In any case, Ruth thought, a bit of re-ordering in old age, a bit of setting things out the way you wanted to remember them was a prerogative; consolation for arthritis and weak eyes. The old lady looked now as if she did not remember having spoken at all, as though she wasn't sure where she was. Ruth turned from her and sliced a rectangle of sponge slab into uniform squares, put a slice onto a white china side-plate decorated with a gold band, and set it on the table beside her.

'Here's some cake,' she said.

Irene's mother accepted the offering by fluttering her fingers, closing her eyes and falling immediately asleep.

Ruth watches her, momentarily envious of that ability of the old, the young and dogs to detach from the actualities of their surroundings, to meet the sandman halfway. She has lain awake these last nights for long enough for the weariness to begin to edge her movements with a rickety indecision, which only she is aware of. She misses Rob, but knows that she doesn't. She knows that she misses some idea of him only; the Rob he was. The Ruth she was. Gone. She picks up the plate of sliced cake to pass it around, though half the bacon sandwiches remain – thick slices of doughy white bread and the bacon just crisped, brown sauce and red on the side, growing cold and greasy and unappetizing despite their initial glory. She has made too many. As she turns with the cake, she almost drops it in her rush to help Lily who, she is distressed to see, is heaving and rolling a large pot containing a larger plant. Ruth knew the plant, but not its name: *ficus benjamina*. It had grown indoors to its present barn-door proportions in the Morning Room, thriving on a happy combination of neglect, infrequent watering and lack of direct draughts.

'Oy,' she shouts. 'You're not to do that on your own.'

Lily, bent double and heaving the poor imprisoned *ficus* with one last charge of her upper body, looks up and sees and hears in Ruth, something. It is Ruth who left the baby hat. It is definitely Ruth who knows. She starts as the urn crashes to its side, more heavily than intended and cracks on the hard stone beneath.

Jason, hearing, comes out and offers to help.

'Lift that up for Lily, Jason,' says Ruth. 'There's a good lad.'

'Might as well leave it there a moment,' says Lily, breaths steadying.

'I am sorry,' says Ruth. She has abandoned the cake and missed the happy sight of Ashley eating a slice behind her. 'Oh, it's broken. I am sorry. I startled you.' She bends and attempts to roll the pot herself, picks up a piece of the shattered rim. There is a stripe of bronze on it that Ruth has never noticed before.

Harry puts down the cake he has lifted on arrival at the humming scene, pleased to be Doing. 'Don't worry,' he says, settling the pot where Lily directs. 'If it was worth anything, I'd have already sold it.' There's no real response to this, so he adds. 'Or broken it. Anyway, nobody's to worry about it. What were you doing with the plant, Lily?'

'She's outgrown her planter,' says Lily. 'I'm going to repot her. I wanted to do it out here to save the rug, but maybe I made the wrong decision.' Her instincts are slowing. Better keep vigilant, she thinks.

Ruth laughs. 'I know that feeling,' she says. And she glances at Lily with I-care, kindness and says, 'I was worried for your back, love.'

'I can manage,' Lily says, though maybe for the first time she thinks she can't and it shows, although not to Jason, who is too young for a reading like that. Nor Harry, who has fetched a brush and pan and is making a fair job of clearing up.

'Can't I help?' says Ruth. 'I've an empathy with things that have grown too big.' Another small, self-conscious laugh.

'Oh,' says Lily, recovering, sliding back into herself as if she has never left. 'The plant isn't too big. It is the pot that is too small.' She stands aside, so that she can let Ruth in to kneel, and help her to free and tease out the bound root ball, and she kneels beside her.

Ruth says nothing, but absorbs this information and its full meaning as it relates to her, because she, sliding back into herself too, senses and just then accepts that it does.

There's Ogden, coming back from market, the following Thursday afternoon. He passes Knot's Lane where Mary always had a fancy to live – wanted a cottage there with fruit trees and a meadow view. Ogden had thought many times of talking to Harry's father about the prospect, but he never had – you've got to seize these moments lest they pass you at a run. Today he has heard of a bullock he's missed – gone in a private deal, cheap enough, to Eddy Webber at Webbery Farm. The loss has made Ogden feel his ageing, his lack of swiftness.

Ogden is sixty-eight now, too old soon for full-time farming without a son for heavy work, for milking hours, he thinks. A farmer needs sons. He and Mary were never blessed. When Harry had come home, Ogden had thought he would maybe hire a bit of young muscle to work the place. Fetch some help in to the cottages, but so far there'd been no help forthcoming. And Harry still talked to Ogden as if he was a young fellow – relied on him.

Ogden, it was true, knew more about the Motthoe land than anyone; knew where the water pipes ran, knew the boundaries. Knew Knot's Lane – a dirt track to anyone else – was called Knot's Lane, though there was no signpost to say so. During the war they had taken the sign posts down in case of invasion – never put half of them back. Irene's mother would know about that, Ogden had heard it from his own mother, God Bless her – all her life at Motthoe, buried in the village church, gentlest soul that ever lived. They were bonded, Irene's mother and Ogden, because their mothers

183

had known each other.

Irene's mother, and *her* mother (Irene's grandmother, then) and Ogden's mother: They'd all helped at Motthoe during those years that none of the men talked ever about when they came home. Ogden's father had come back silent, stayed that way through his farming life. Not a bad man, not unkind, but silent, all the men were. The war years, not Ogden's years, but passed to him – inherited, still undiluted. Irene's mother had lived them. Lived them at Motthoe. There were things they knew, that generation. Not like Harry. He was no chip off the block.

But then, Ogden thought, pulling the car he rarely drove into the lane, that was maybe no bad thing either; the old boy, Harry's father, had been a tartar for years. Since, Ogden realized, just then, with a small, jarring dazzle of recognition, the old man's wife – Harry's mother – had died.

Ogden was surprised, pulling up at his cottage, to see one of the objects of his thoughts, Harry, in his porch, sitting on the drooping stoop. He stood when Ogden approached.

'How have you got on then?' he said. They had discussed the bullock, though Ogden had not marked any enthusiasm in Harry. He was struck now that something was keening up in the lad. Maybe make a land man of him after all.

'I lost the bullock,' he said.

'I expect there will be others,' Harry said.

''Spect there will,' said Ogden. They smiled.

Harry stepped away from the porch to let Ogden pass.

'I won't keep you,' Harry said. 'I just wanted to go over some things and… well, perhaps if there is a convenient time.'

'There's never a time like now,' Ogden said. 'If you don't

mind waiting while I put the stove up, we can have a cup of tea.'

'I don't mind at all,' Harry said. 'If you don't.'

'Not at all,' said Ogden. He didn't. He was curious to see what was twitching in the man.

By the time Harry leaves Ogden's cottage, he has a glancing knowledge of the number of acres under plow, the rotations (four year; roots, corn, corn, grass), the profit possible from each, and Ogden's preferred cattle breeds. They have talked the benefits of sheep. He has been appraised of routines and systems and machinery. He knows the gate at the far west road entrance is in need of repair and has agreed to meet Ogden there tomorrow. Harry is marching to the sound of a rallying cry.

Ruth's routine is set orderly now; girls to school, cleaning, cooking, more cleaning, a short break in Lily's garden, back to school to fetch the girls, finish the cleaning, more cooking. She likes it. It's as if she has been doing it all her life. The girls are getting on better – their teachers say they're sitting quieter; homework is in on time. Jess is less dozy in the afternoons. All good, thinks Ruth, all worth it. When she is waiting for them at the street they've designated as invisible enough in the afternoons, she looks at her phone and wills it to ring. Wants to hear Rob's voice say: I've licked the drinking. Let's start over.

The phone does not ring.

She drives back to Motthoe this afternoon with the girls

bickering over some nonsense she doesn't tune into and pulls in behind Jason – up for the grass, steady worker that he is.

Jason gets out of the driver's side of his Dad's car and skirts the rear of it with a serious face. Always has a serious face. He opens the passenger side and holds up a warning finger, then he takes the hand of a small boy and talks stern and quiet to him. The little one is a chip off the older, peas in a pod. The little one, though, is not quiet. He's whizzing his head about like a mechanism with a fault, and the one arm not pinned by his big brother is thrashing. The middle part of the child swings wildly at the hips – side to side, side to side. He growls, tugging the held hand almost free, but Jason doesn't let go and he starts to scream. Something in that scream pierces, like the howl of a wounded thing. Jason lifts his head. Not up but back, tilts his head back and looks at the sky, entreating.

The little one is still screaming when Ruth walks up to him and says, 'Cookies in this bag for a quiet boy.'

The screaming cuts. The lip-line sets and the eyes focus.

The arm in Jason's grip releases, but Jason does not relax at all.

'Will you come with me?' Ruth says not quite meeting the boy's eyes, standing back just enough. Giving him air. 'We'll have a cookie in the kitchen while Jason cuts the grass.'

The boy stops screaming and the birdsong is sweet in the new silence.

'You gotta watch...' Jason says in a pulled-back voice.

'Yep,' says Ruth, she's got it. She switches her hand for Jason's in the child's. 'He'll be fine... you get on.' And the little chap begins to walk with her toward the house. Over her shoulder, she calls. 'You girls change into your jeans and see what Lily needs doing.'

And the girls do it and leave off arguing because the boy's sudden quiet is like a blanket over the afternoon.

Jason calls out, 'He doesn't talk. His name is Callum.'

'Callum,' repeats Ruth. Then she says, 'Seems to me we got more than enough talkers in the world already, Callum.'

Callum just keeps walking – a short-strided, high-toed walk that requires all of his concentration.

After the cookies, Ruth takes Callum with her to change Irene's mother's bed. He makes a pile of the dirty linens and sits on it serious as a gnome, follows her expressionless to the bathroom and watches her spray the enamel with a foaming cleaner and bend to wipe it off, backs himself against the wall when she turns the taps on to rinse.

'Don't you worry, sweetie, just a bit of water.' She turns the faucets down and drips the water on to a sponge.

Callum smiles at the sponge and then at her, face transformed.

Dear little chap, thinks Ruth. Little chap inside there. All goes on well until the vacuum cleaner, which she has let him hold, is knocked on and the roar sets him screaming again and wind-milling and shaking all over. Ruth shuts the machine off with her toe and runs to him. He has cornered himself, shrunken. She sits in the corner with him. Sits and waits till the screaming turns to sobs and then weeping and then panting, short heaving breaths from the baby chest. Then she reaches a hand out and he takes it.

'We'll have a look outside now, shall we Callum?' she says.

Jason has finished the grass and is sorting pallets for

Lily. His face clouds when he sees Ruth with Callum, 'Trouble?' he asks.

'None,' says Ruth. She sits Callum on a pallet, lets him scrabble his hands in the dirt below it.

Jason watches and sits beside him. 'The woman who looks after him moved away,' he says. 'Mum doesn't get home from work till 6:30.'

'Falls to you, then?'

'Yes,'

'How's that working out?'

'I've got college work and here…not as if you can leave him alone.'

'No,' says Ruth.

Jason reaches to help Callum, but Callum pushes his hand away and the out-of-kilter look hits his eyes again. Jason raises his hands, 'Okay,' he says.

'Tell your mother I'm available,' says Ruth. 'If she's looking. I can bring him here with me, three days. How'd that be, do you think?'

'I'll tell her,' says Jason. 'I'll tell her.' Jumps to his work again, light with relief.

Jason and Callum's mum up on the weekend to check the arrangement. And there is Callum, sorting Lily's seed trays into sizes, subdued and abstracted. His mother strokes his hair from his face, but he doesn't look up. Ruth watching her own girls; kidding and teasing and bedding in tiny plants, just like Lily had shown them, recognizes the pains of this mother and thinks: It is us, the mothers, we've got to stick together.

Seth had lovely eyes. His Ma said that of him, first time he was locked up. He was a lovely kid, she said. Not like his brother. Ma had always figured the brother for the wrong'un; such a fussy baby, never slept, something cold about him, chip off his bastard, battering father. She'd given up on him from the start. But Seth, her second, easy as you like, slept well, ate everything you gave him, sweet little kid. Didn't turn till he was about nine – maybe it was the brother's influence . Running about the town with a rough bunch, up to all sorts. Her getting the phone calls – shoplifting, vandalism. Then just sixteen, Seth turned over an off-licence. Thirty-two quid for his trouble and as many cans as he could carry. The cops had cornered him in three hours, belching drunk in some fella's bedsit.

On the way home from court Seth's Ma had cried, cried for her two lost boys, both banged up now. Gone home to her three younger ones, new dad, new life, and said, don't you lot put me through this, I haven't got it in me.

Seth never thought of his mother. Seth didn't think. Seth didn't speak, unless it was to himself. That had started as a way to keep them at bay – do-gooders and nine-to-fivers who thought they had solutions in their heads. Thought he was looking for one. They made it hard to keep to yourself. You had to keep sly, keep foxy, keep your head down. If you took the tow path and came across a middle-ager, walking her dog, exercising her sagging buttocks, scarf at her neck and lipstick on her thinning lips – like anybody cared – if you happened to come across her, despite having picked the quietest of mornings on a gray November day, you kept your eyes down. She would stand straighter on passing, pull the useless excuse for an animal in on its leash. She would brisk her pace – scared. Man alone. Man walking. Man wearing an army great coat and a couple of days beard growth. He didn't catch her eye, because he wanted to be forgotten and he did not want to see his reflection in it.

But now the talking had crept up on him. He didn't know if he was doing it or not, half the time. Walking, dossing in outhouses, eyes wandering for eggs, berries in his hand, swimming from time to time in rivers – sometimes he was talking, wording things to himself without knowing it. He only realized when he stopped, when the pittery birdsong took over again. The voices had stopped. Maybe they were not in his head after all. Maybe the involuntary working of his jaw had made them.

He was drawn to railway tracks and walked them often. He knew the abandoned ones and he knew the live ones – he thought of lying down on those, thought of it many times, but he had something to do first. He had something to do. They never thought of that, the sorts who wanted to cage you in a nasty room – brick wall views and sounds of babies howling, piss stink in the elevator. They didn't think you had something on your mind. They thought you wanted a job painting furniture, a job on an assembly line. Thought you wanted to pay for your own roaring Friday nights.

For a long time, Seth had found solace in drink, but two

years he'd gone now without even that. Maybe he was crazy. Maybe he was going mad. Mad as Paul the banker – lost his job, lost his Mrs, lost his home, lost his life, lived under a viaduct for fourteen years. Mad Paul, the banker. Seth didn't know if he was crazy, didn't care either. He didn't need to look in the trim, dog-walking woman's ordinary face to see his lunacy reflected. He had something to do, just the one thing. And when he'd done it, he could lie down and listen for his own end.

His feet, steady and meditative, walked the lane. He reached without pausing and plucked a frill of honeysuckle from the high edging bank and crushed it in his hand.

It was a miniature noose, made of copper wire. Half a yard of it coiled in Ogden's other hand.

'Found it hooked over a snare on the far side of Ash Ridge.'

'Keep an eye out,' says Harry.

Irene overhears this conversation and realizes love has made her sloppy. She must do her rounds, remember her duties. She chastises herself for her neglect.

Lily overhears this conversation and the electric part of her flicks alive. She realizes she has not been vigilant. She has let her defenses slip. She chastises herself for staying in one place for far too long.

CHAPTER NINE

It wasn't hard to get in, the door wasn't locked. It wasn't as if there was anything to steal. Dan's quarters: a loft. There was enough room for a double bed, a desk, a chest of drawers, a wardrobe, a bedside cabinet and two armchairs. One of the dogs had followed her. He scaled one of the armchairs, curled into it and looked at her. She walked over to him and momentarily cupped his chin in her hand.

Above the chairs was a skylight and above that the night – clouds obscuring the moon. On one side if the room there was an arched window, similarly open to the dark, no curtain.

Jess was surprised to see that it offered a view of the driveway and the walk to Lily's cottage. She hadn't thought of that – Dan could see down from here. Perhaps he had watched Jess and her sister getting out of the car after school, or helping Lily lug supplies, while their Mum cleaned inside.

The room was very tidy. Tidier than Jess's room. Her room at home she was thinking of, not the one here at Motthoe, which wasn't her proper room and was made anyway hellish by having to share with Ashley. Jess missed home. If Motthoe hadn't had Dan in it, she'd have run away. Dan had a painting on one wall, a big one, with stripes going across. Jess decided immediately that she liked it, just as much as Dan obviously did. On the wall opposite the arched window a door led to a narrow corridor with a bathroom on one side and a small, orderly kitchen on the other. Jess didn't go in, she wasn't here to poke around, to invade Dan's privacy, or upset him in any way. Jess was here because she loved Dan and she wanted him to know it.

In the armchair the dog, whose name was Gumbo, had settled his head into his crossed front paws. He watched Jess undress and fold her clothes. She laid them uncharacteristically precisely on the other chair. When she climbed into bed, he made a low noise in the back of his throat, satiny as one of his own ears, and went back to sleep.

Whatever it was that Lily heard, crossing to Ashcott, it wasn't a fox. There was very little moon, but rather than shine her torch about looking for the source of the sound she turned it off. She had walked out of the gate, by the garage, past Dan's upstairs flat with its blinking windows, along the chalky lane. The dirt road surface had been flattened by an earlier shower, the air was still soft with it. A fine mist of drizzle dampened her hair. Her feet made no sound, but something had. Like a breath.

Lily began the rhythmic inner mantra that she had been practicing for years: nothing to be truly feared, nothing. Keep moving. For all those years she had been jumping at shadows and then, effortful, convincing herself they were shadows, telling herself that they were, showing herself that they were. She knew that they were. But there was always a delay, a nimbus of anxiety always engulfed her for a period between knowing and accepting. Sometimes it lasted days; days when searing flame heat would not have been tangible to her, when the edge of a razor against her skin would have imparted no sensation, days when she was numb with terror. During these spells she saw phantoms in every shadow, in every outline of every bush, in every sudden take-off of every bird. She heard demons cackle in every spin of tyres on gravel, in every creak of every door. She knew this and knew, too, that these nightmares always dissolved eventually in the calm of dull explanation, but, nevertheless, when she saw the shape on the far side of the sloping remains of cob wall – a shape shrouded to its knees by ghostly cocksfoot – after she had heard that sound, that breath of something near, she believed that it was a man.

Jess couldn't quite decide how to arrange herself. She repositioned a pillow at her neck. She sat up a way and tucked one arm behind her head, but it felt silly. She lowered the arm. She leaned forward and shook her hair about. She had nice hair, everybody said so. Nice, thick, warm brown hair. She had washed it this evening, stood a long time under the water, creaking from the worn shower fitting. Lily had given her some shampoo, with rosemary in it. It smelled good. Surprisingly, so did Dan's pillows. Not like Man. Not like Jess's Dad's pillow smelled sometimes, of beer and sweat, but clean and lineny. Like the piles of washing Jess's mum ferried about at the big house. Maybe her mum had washed these sheets, Jess thought. Probably she had. The thought unsettled her. She didn't want to be thinking of her mum just now. Jess had checked that Ruth was well asleep before she'd snuck out, and Ashley too, the snitch. But still.

She tucked herself further down into the sheets. She'd been surprised that Dan wasn't there. He might have gone into town, she supposed. She didn't want him to have gone into town. She knew what her Dad got like when he went into town. She didn't think Dan was a drinker, but you never knew. That was the kind of thing her Mum said: you never can tell. There's all sorts behind closed doors.

Now Jess was behind a closed door.

Gumbo sniffed and twitched, fetching pheasants in his sleep. Jess tensed and willed Dan to come back, soon. She loved him so much. Although, in his bed, carrying out the plan she'd cooked up in her head these past two weeks, actually doing it. She was nervous. She wished he had been there when she'd arrived. If he had been there, she'd be in his arms by now. He'd be smiling at her and kissing her. She was going to make him happy. Dan. Dan who looked so sad. She, Jess, was going to love him happy. And she'd be happy, too. She'd escape her schoolgirl bed, and her schoolgirl life and move in here, into this flat above the garage, and sleep with him in these sheets every night. And, in the mornings, she'd do all the tidying up.

Lurches at every sound, every imagined footfall, kept Jess awake until 11:45. Twenty minutes later when Dan came in, he found her there, curled like an ammonite and sound asleep.

Dan had come in quiet. Boots left below, as was his habit. He had caught regulation from his mother and had it compounded at school, and then, bachelored young, he'd stuck it – come to like it. Gumbo looked up and gave a half-eyed look to him, and Dan for a moment wondered how he'd left him shut in. Then he turned and saw Jess in his bed. She was asleep in the bottomless, careless way that only the very young ever are. Her hair fell across her forehead and her upper body was bared above the sheet. Her lips were slightly parted, but her breathing was soundless. She was as beautiful a thing as Dan had ever come home to. He stared a moment, both in shock and wonder, in the way a dreamer does when woken – at their own ceiling, their own limbs. The sense of being in the wrong place despite the logic and familiarity of the surroundings struck him. He felt as though he had opened the wrong door in a hotel – come to a room exactly the same as his, but not his. Another world from his. He searched momentarily for reasonable explanations for Jess's presence – an overflow of sleepers in the main house.

Unlikely, extremely unlikely. He glanced about for Ruth, or the younger one, Ashley, the sister. He saw neither, evidence of neither. There on the chair, though, the neatly folded pile of clothes. The heartbreakingly pretty bra on top.

Jess rolled then. Dan froze. Jess opened her eyes and smiled him a smile that gift-wrapped all explanation. She sat up, just slightly, tipped forward on her elbows, her hair falling back to the pillows she'd pulled under her head. She looked like a mermaid, a goddess, an offering.

Dan, turned and fled back down the stairs. He heard Gumbo bark and Jess call after him.

Dan considered fetching Ruth, but felt somehow that this was the wrong course. Irene might know what to do, but she would be asleep now in the dressing room off her mother's room, if she was at Motthoe at all and not – of all of them the luckiest – somewhere else, nestled in perfect, available love. He could just leave the girl, there were plenty of places to sleep undetected at Motthoe, he could curl up somewhere and hope she'd be gone in the morning. But she might not be. He could tell Harry. But what would Harry have to contribute? How could Harry extricate Dan from whatever jam he was in? Dan felt instinctively that he was in a jam and that he needed extricating. He had a strong urge to establish his innocence in the situation immediately, before any possible taint could stick. He knew, really, that there was only one person who could help him, but he didn't want to startle her either. Then Jess came to the door. He heard her plaintive call of his name again and he walked briskly across the gravel and down the path that led to Ashcott. Lily might be awake, she kept erratic hours. Like he did. And if a light was on, he could shout to her.

Forewarn her, it was only him, Dan.

No lights were on.

Lily had never swum up from sleep. Always the difference, the moment that divided conscious from unconscious had been lightning brief, to the extent that she often felt that she had never been asleep at all. Often, she hadn't. She slept the way a cat does with one ear half perked for prey or predators. As a child she had been woken in the night many times by her mother, intentionally, unintentionally. She could still feel that sticky, boozy breath, in her ear, over her face. Her mother kissing her, 'I love you, Lily. I'd do anything for you,' she'd say, before she dropped comatose on to her back, like something beached, pinning Lily to the wall of whatever bedroom she was calling home. But then in the morning, smoking in the kitchen, her eyes would be cool. Hurry up, she'd say, you'll be late. Just like a normal mother, the normal mother she passed for, just often enough. Just often enough to keep Lily out of care. Not like Angie – Lily's friend for six months when they were five. Angie had gone into care, then got fostered. Lily thought Angie had disappeared, thought she'd been kidnapped by wolves. Lily's mother had reminded her of the ghost of Angie often. Not like poor Angie, off living who knows where, with God knows who, she'd say. Lily was lucky with a mother to look after her. I do everything for you, Lily. Drunk hot breath on Lily's face, keeping her awake.

Lily had kept the light sleeping habit into adulthood. Preferred to doze, half sleeps sustained her. Her pregnancy naps, her greenhouse and garden sleeps had been deepening, but at night her unconscious still roved only the shallow spaces. Tonight, she had not slept at all and intuited a man's soundless presence before it made the cottage gate – always kept closed because it squeaked with movement. One more alarm in a complex system of sound traps that Lily had laid, had laid everywhere she'd lived for the last fourteen years. She could hear her own breathing, fast and shallow. This is it, she thought. She had known it was coming when she'd heard the breathing in the lane. Known he had found her. She was in the van's driver seat. It was parked as it was always was, facing out, down to the lane. She turned the engine over and drove.

At first, Ogden had talked to her, to the spirit of her; what did she reckon to this, or that? Sat in his chair, or the side of his bed, talking to her, like a madman, like a crazy person, saying the words out loud: Well now, Mary, what do you say? Sometimes, in those first years, he had heard her talk back – clear as a goose call on a summer night. But after a while it had got dimmer – that sense of her – and that was when he'd started heading for the Dog and Duck when his work was done. He went right down there in whatever vehicle he was driving, straight off the field and into the car park at the side there. He'd had a hell of a job getting back up some nights.

But lately he hasn't gone down there so much. Hasn't needed to. He is thinking this, coming up the lane on foot tonight. This has been his first night in the Dog and Duck for months, the months since Lily come. He is really not drunk – only time for a swift couple, just made his quiet way along the lane, no desperation in it. He has taken the track through the woods to the village, he has enjoyed it. The same walk he did to school as a nipper. No school there now, what kids there are out here get bussed over to Moorstead.

He has turned out of the woods path into the narrow part of the road – not a road, only him and Irene ever on it. It is pitch dark under the cloud cover. Ogden is alone with the night and his thoughts. He hears the engine well before it is visible, and flattens himself to the hedge, but there is no space there at the bend, so he shouts as Lily's van comes into view. Slow down. But the van comes fast and reckless and Ogden leaps and clambers the hedge – three hundred years dense and high. He scratches himself and is bleeding when he leaps over into the ditch.

Tis Harry pulls him out and behind him Our Girl, Our Lily, is there, so Ogden is not sure at first who had been driving. It was Lily.

'You can't run forever,' says Harry.

He has brought Lily back to the house. Lily has not even come round enough, come out of the fog in her head enough, to register this – that she has come back, that he has successfully stopped her, at least for now, from deserting Motthoe, from running away. She is still in the lather of fright. It is the baby inside her, too, the off-centeredness of things, the vulnerability her big belly gives her. She is like a spinning top, middle heavy. If she slows down, she leans, she falls. Lily is not accustomed to this lack of autonomy, lack of control over her own doings. She has let Harry bring her back with no more than an elbow hold, mind too blank for wondering why he was there. He put his hand on her arm and turned her around and got into her van and drove her back to Motthoe – left Ogden with the jeep. Poor Ogden, she is pricked into her surroundings by this thought. She had almost run him down.

'Is Ogden injured?' she said.

'He's not.'

They'd returned the way she'd left, how long before, ten minutes? Two hours? Something in between – she'd reached the downhill lane that meets up with the main road at the bottom, she'd have turned after that. She looked up. Harry had heated milk and put it in a mug. He put it on the table beside her. Warm milk.

'I had a nanny, once, swore by warm milk for all eventualities: shock, bee stings, death.' He nudged the cup towards her and she picked it up.

'I don't love you, Harry,' Lily said. She said it gauzy-voiced, though, as if she did. She lifted the milk to her lips and wished that she did. Life would be simpler in many ways if she could just love Harry. Settle in with him and dream some of his dreams. If she could stop running.

'I know that,' says Harry. Not sounding such a dreamer.

'I've no reason not to,' she said. 'Not in you, I mean. I just...' She is a carer rather than a lover. Lily has cared for and enjoyed some men, but never for long. She loves in the way she sleeps, lightly and evanescently, because, after the first tremble of novelty has passed, she cannot bear to be touched, kissed, fondled by even the gentlest of them.

'I know,' says Harry again. He sits across from her. His back is straight and his shoulders are squared. He looks right at her. 'I think maybe I have some of that in me, too,' he says.

'Of what?' she says remotely.

'That wall-building thing that stops you finding love.'

Lily put her cup down, but didn't speak. She couldn't have.

'I started building my wall when my mother died,' Harry said. 'And kept at it during what came after – the feeling of being different…and alone, I guess.' He stood up. She watched him lift the milk pan and rinse it under the tap. 'But now I'm becoming aware of that – of those barriers,' he said, his back to her. The water splashed into the sink. He turned the tap off again and turned and leaned against the counter. 'They're losing their density. It's an uncomfortable process sometimes – like opening yourself to a cold wind, but there's a bit of sunshine, too. I feel stronger, somehow. In myself.'

'I think you are…' Lily said. Surer, she was thinking.

He walked past her and rounded the table, drying his hands on a paper towel – so endearing, the small ordinariness of it. He took his seat opposite her again.

'But I suspect that your wall is thicker than mine, Lily,' he said. 'Because it has had to be. I think your wall was built to keep out real pain. I have watched you, and seen that in you, Lily. Your powerful need for self-protection…and I wish I could erase it and whatever caused it. And if that is love, then love is what I feel for you.'

Lily the Tiller lifts her head to the dear face of Harry, Lord of Dreams; his blue eyes to her brown ones, his heart

pinned outside of him, bared, for her to see – for her. And
she knows that this is the moment to tell him that for almost
year during her early teens – when she was younger than Jess,
younger than Ashley – her feckless mother took the lecher,
Seth Banbury into her bed and Seth Banbury left that bed
whenever he had a mind to for Lily's. She could tell him that
it is this vileness she runs from, this man, who despite his
merciful arrest in a pub brawl and subsequent imprisonment
when she was fourteen, found her twice – once when she
was sixteen, and again at eighteen – and made no attempt to
speak to her, but watched her, and let her see him watching,
so that she knew. And could not forget. It is ten years now
since she saw him last. Ten years of knowing he is probably
dead, decomposing unmourned somewhere. Lily knows that
it is a ghost she runs from, has run from again tonight. But
her memories are alive, and more real to her than anything in
this kitchen, than anything in the world. Only her gardening,
only her trick of letting nature and its charms envelop her,
swallow her up, keeps them cornered. But now the caressing
gentleness of Harry's expression has a muting effect, too, on
their vividness.

Then, *No*, she thinks, *no*. Love, the clasp, the ongoing grip
of it, is still too frightening a concept for her.

Harry sees this last in her face. 'I don't think it is so much
about not loving people,' he says with feather softness. 'I
think it's more about not knowing how to be loved.'

'Maybe I don't want to be loved,' Lily says, voice still
coming from the stars. 'Can't be.'

Harry judges that he should not argue. He does not want
to goad the conversation to the pass – the narrow single exit

point where she will have to tell him out loud, in order to move on, that her heart belongs to another, to her child's father. Even Harry knows this now. That there is a child to come. He says evenly, 'Lily, you can only run so far, till you start coming back. I learned that. I tried to run away from this.' A hand, palm up, circled the room. 'I don't think – I don't know what you are running from, or to and don't presume it is the same, but...'

'They give for rain,' said Lily. She finished the milk. Outside trees sighed, a breeze was coming up.

'For your garden,' said Harry, letting her lead.

'It's your garden, Harry,' said Lily.

'No. It's yours now.' He reached across and laid the very tip of his ring finger on the tip of hers, the tiniest and most affecting of touches. 'Lily, you've brought life to Motthoe. That is something I have wanted to do for a long time and failed at consistently. I do think of you... in a romantic way. But that is not the only reason I followed you this evening.'

He had followed her, then. She gave a small nod, recognizing this.

'It is true that I didn't want you to leave without knowing what you mean to me, but that wasn't the only reason I wanted to bring you back,' he said. 'I want you here, Lily, I want you to stay, because of the greenness you have brought to us all. You brought a spring that was a long time coming. Stay, Lily, not just for me, but for Motthoe, and the people here. And also, and this may be presumptuous, but maybe for yourself. Give yourself a break, quit the road for a bit and take it easy. There are no demands on you here. Make a life, for yourself. And...' he said.

*And...*So it was all about known; the baby. One of her secrets outed. No hiding at Motthoe.

It was the next day when she knew for sure she had invented him: the dark shadow that stalked her – that she had turned him brawn with her thoughts alone. It had been Dan she'd heard. Dan who'd shouted her name after the van, so that Harry, who'd been talking with him most of that evening, and had taken a notion after he'd left, to walk a while before he went to bed, and whose fancy had taken him, as it often did, in the direction of Lily, heard the shout, and the engine, and ran automatically for the jeep, parked with the keys in it a hundred yards behind him.

Dan explained all this, a picture painted clearly in daylight, when he found Lily in the afternoon, deadheading with her skirt waistband pulled up so that the fabric fell like a dress over her thickening mid-section. Dan had sought her out, he wanted guidance.

'She's just a girl,' he told Lily. 'And vulnerable. I don't want to encourage her...but I don't know how not to without – I don't know what to say. It's hard to shake her off when we're all living here, and, anyway she's a nice kid...and Ruth's so... I just don't want to add to what they're dealing with...' He has his palms up, open.

For the second time in twenty-four hours Lily sees a man unguarded, caring, protective. There are men like that. People like that. Once again it renders her speechless, this knowledge. She stares away into the woods.

'Sorry, I'm rambling. It's not your problem…it's not even a problem, I just…'

Lily saw Dan's dilemma, though she had marveled at it – at his coming to find her. To set the situation right. Clear thinking, she thought, given the other directions the situation could have gone in. All the other directions. Lily thought of the girl, Jess – Ruth's child and a child to everyone else, even Dan, Thank God. Thought of her slipping herself into Dan's bed, voluntarily. And Dan leaving her there alone, voluntarily. So many directions it could have gone.

'You don't want to hurt her feelings,' Lily said.

'No, I guess that's right.'

'You don't want to hurt her.'

'No…'

'You did the right thing, Dan.'

'I feel like a fool. Nothing really happened – some kid got a notion into her head, that's all, nothing happened, and yet I feel as though there's more, I don't know, more to it and I want to get it right.'

'You did get it right.'

'I thought maybe – I know it's a cop out – but would you talk to her?'

'Yes.'

'Thank you,'

She turned to him and smiled, but it was not her usual smile. The day was cold, there had been a mist in the morning, and now a strangely autumnal feeling had crept into it and in to Lily's face, some change. Dan had only heard the gist of the night before's excursion. Lily had been rattled by something, by him creeping up like that – he'd apologized.

But it did not explain completely the way she had taken off.

'Are you all right, Lily?'

She sat forward, put her arms across her chest. 'Yes,' she said. 'I am.'

When Dan had gone, Lily took a bucket and filled it from the stand pipe, she removed her cardigan but not her dress-worn skirt. She lifted the bucket high above her head and tipped it over her herself. The cold rush of the water made her gasp.

'You're gone,' she said out loud in that moment of baptism. 'You're dead to the world and to me. I have a new life inside me, and a new life of my own. And I can live it. I am free.'

Lily walked out of her garden and over the field with the wet skirt clinging to the bulge she would no longer disguise, back to Ashcott; home. She took her things from her van – the smell inside, in the past so comforting, unappealing now. She walked up the path and into the cottage. There was a latch on the front door but she did not lock it behind her. In the kitchen there was a larder with a cold shelf and a small north facing window, she opened that and left the larder door open. She opened the sitting room windows and door. Air began to circulate through the house.

She ran water for a bath. The bathroom walls had the same aged, tan sheen as the kitchen ceiling. The window looked out onto woods at the back and she stood a moment checking them for signs of life. She saw none, though she knew they seethed with it. It was a particular kind of life she was habitually watchful for and she reminded herself now that she no longer would be. When the bath was run she stepped into it and sunk in. Her head rested on the curve at the tub's back, and the ends of her hair swum around her.

After her bath she went into Ashcott's main bedroom, to the bed in which she had never spent a night. She spread her bedding things on it, lay down on them and went to sleep for nineteen hours.

In the morning, when she woke, fine, dawn light coming in through the latticed windows to her left, she lay a moment and looked around. She knew that many country people had lived in cottages like these all their lives, been born into them and died in them. Women had given birth to their own children in the same pitched ceilinged rooms where their mothers had birthed them. What would it be like to know, to know with absolute certainty where you would be fifty years from now, ten years from now? Tomorrow?

She is the opposite of me because she's restless, Dan writes. You can see it in her all the time. She's always moving somehow, not fidgety, but moving definitely like wheat in a field. Sometimes when she's standing, talking, or looking at the garden, which she does a lot, with a really watchful expression on her face – as if it might get up and move with her – she sways. Today she was really good about the girl.

She is beautiful the girl, Jess, and some twerp is going to come sniffing around her soon enough and I will be jealous. I am more flattered than I like to think about at the fact that she considered me. I felt so bad, rejecting her that way, and worse for having thought about not doing it.

Harry was off with me this morning – probably thought

I was at Lily's cottage last night for the same reason he was. Poor old Harry. Here I am living with him, living off him half the time, and he never complains. Now he thinks I am after his girl. I am not, I'll tell him. Not why, not that Lily is too hurt inside for the lumbering likes of me, but I'll tell him he is better suited for her. Harry is good, all through. But still, he is beginning to see that there are some people who are bringers and others who are takers – like me. I am wondering whether, when the scales fall completely from his eyes, he will ask me to leave. No doubt he'll come up with some plan to turn the coach house into holiday cottages, or monkey houses and will want me out. I am the opposite of Lily because the thought of moving, of uprooting myself from Motthoe is painful to me.

Ruth had intended simply to leave the things (a Moses basket, some blankets, four white sleepsuits, a pair of knitted bootees) and to check on Lily. It was odd her having left the garden so early the day before. Irene and Ruth wanted to check on her in the afternoon when she didn't come up to the house, but Harry, overhearing them, had said, No – with an authority that had set their faces to him and quietened their talk.

'Leave her be,' he said. 'She'll come when it suits her.'

Dan said he'd seen her already, talked to her. She seemed tired.

'The baby,' Irene's mother said from her chair. 'The nurse one is having a baby.'

Ruth glanced quickly at Irene, who turned to her mother. Dan saw the glance and so did Harry. Nobody spoke, nobody felt they could talk of Lily's baby (the baby they had all seen glimpses of, and never colored in) – unless she did first. It felt, somehow, disloyal. A betrayal.

'The nurse one,' said Irene's mother. 'With the gentle hands.'

'Yes, mother,' Irene said.

Her mother smiled at her. It was not a smile that acknowledged, or recognized, or communicated. It was a smile that came from inside something, from behind something, something that separated the smiler from everything, from everyone. Then Irene's mother's face became utterly still, her eyes absent of all connection. The smile ossified.

'Mother?' Irene said, moving to her side. She kneeled and put one hand on her mother's knee. 'Mother?' she said again.

Irene's mother seemed to shake a little, a leaf, then, slowly, she looked at Irene. Her expression was blank.

'Are you feeling all right?' Irene said.

'Yes,' said her mother, from somewhere far, far away.

Irene had called Dr Galbraith – Jason and Callum's father – and he had come to the house. It might have been a small stroke he'd said, but it might not have been. By the time he'd arrived, Irene's mother had been sharpened up again – enough to tell him she had no interest in doctors, enough to chide Irene for calling one. But the fuss of it had taken up the afternoon, and, as instructed, they had left Lily to herself. After supper Ruth had fetched out the baby things from her room in the Nanny Flat. She'd bought them two weeks before – enjoyed going to the baby shop, enjoyed the chat with the sales assistant, picked out what she'd wanted and paid for it with a ripple of pleasure. A baby. One day she could do this for her own girls. One sunny day.

It was about 7:00 a.m. when she put the basket on the doorstep of Lily's cottage where she would find them, but then she wondered if Lily was using the cottage, or whether she was still half living in her van. She hoped not. Lily needed proper rest now. She looked up and saw that Ashcott's windows were open and thought she heard someone moving about. She set off again along the path, up the track, back to Motthoe, back to rustle her girls. But then she thought, *I hope one of the barn cats doesn't settle itself in the Moses basket*, and doubled back again and found Lily standing, looking down at it with an expression that seemed more disturbed than delighted. I got that wrong, thought Ruth. Damn.

'Lily,' she called from the gate.

Lily bounced her head up and shoved the Moses basket with her foot, as if in an attempt to slide it behind her, but even as she did, her movements slowed and her eyes calmed again, she became her usual self. It was just Ruth, Ruth who had put the things there. Dear Ruth.

Ruth came through the gate and closed it behind her with care, she had a sense of the way other people did things. Maybe it came from cleaning other people's houses, or maybe that was just what made her so good at it – her natural respect for the practices of others, their ways. Lily always kept her gate closed. Ruth knew that. She walked up the path. She asked if she might come in.

'Please do,' said Lily.

Ruth took off her shoes and bent to lift the Moses basket. She carried it to Lily's kitchen and put it on the table. It was warm and clean in there. There were others in far worse situations whose babies came out all right, she thought.

'I'm sorry I startled you,' she said.

Lily didn't know what to say yet, so she busied herself filling the kettle. She set it on the stove element to warm, and opened the door and riddled the ashes through. The heat was reflected in her cheeks when she closed it again and turned back to Ruth. She put the poker in the bucket in the corner.

'I should have said something first,' said Ruth. 'But you didn't seem ready to talk.'

'Yes,' said Lily. The first word she'd spoken, not just today, but on this subject at all. The first time she'd said anything in the presence of another that openly acknowledged her baby. It was therefore not a word, but a speech.

Ruth gave it the long and deep reverence it deserved. Then she said, 'Have you seen a doctor at all, Lily?'

'No,' said Lily – her second speech on the subject.

Ruth digested both. 'Do you think you ought to, love?'

Her voice was kind, and low, and tear-drawing. Lily felt the pull of it. Ruth reached out a hand and waited. Lily looked up at her eventually as if waiting for direction, for instruction. Behind her the kettle steamed and whistled and Ruth stood and made them both tea from the rose hips Lily kept in a blue and white bowl. The cottage reminded Ruth of the one her grandmother had lived in down by the river, vegetable garden at the back, view of the apple trees, baking in the pantry and condensation inside the upstairs windows for six months of the year. She remembered putting her hand to the condensation as a child to melt it. She passed Lily her cup and took her seat again.

'There's no right time for a baby to come, Lily,' she said.

Lily looked at her again with those advice-hungry eyes, so she went on. 'There's no right time. They come and you build your life around them. And it's not like they're born and then it's Job Done. It's not like that – things keep on happening. Once you have a child in your life, any control you had – if you ever did have any mind...Anyways, any control you had over things is gone. They bring their own package with them, kids. And you adapt. It comes to you... Not easily always, but naturally. You figure out how to give them what they need, what they want. You do everything you can with whatever you've got. And sometimes you get it mighty wrong and sometimes you don't. And sometimes you get some help and sometimes you don't. But they grow up anyway, and mostly they're okay. So long as you love them. That's the only time, I reckon, when you really shouldn't have them – if you think you can't love them. Really can't love them. And there are people, I think, mothers and fathers, who fall into that category. But I wouldn't have thought you did, Lily. I've seen you with my girls, and young Callum. Seen the patience in you, and the caring. I reckon that'd be a blessing to any child. A gift. Don't think about the timing. Don't think about the man. You just get on and be a mother, love your baby. The rest will come.'

Lily who had not taken her eyes from Ruth throughout this, smiled at her now, though tears were in her eyes. She was being given permission, by a decent person, with nothing to gain, by a good decent caring woman, to go ahead and have a child of her own, and to love it. It was the kindest thing anyone had done for Lily in her life. She let the tears fall. Maybe, she thought, it all needs to come out now. Maybe I need to shed, like a maple in autumn, to make way for new growth.

Jess had cried watching Dan walking away. He'd been walking fast. She'd sunk back from the window with the awful realization of his rejection. His not wanting her any more than the Layabout Boy had. Nobody wanted her, she was that unattractive. Then she had thought, dressing, maybe, if she could just talk to him, she could make him see. What a good couple they would make. He hadn't thought of that before, probably. She'd surprised him. She berated herself for that. For getting it wrong. She was for ever getting it wrong. She got her clothes on and ran back to the Nanny Flat with her shoes in her hand, crept past her sleeping mother's door, past her snoring sister's bed and got into her own single, kid's bed and wept. Then today she'd hung out at the wood end of Lily's garden.

When Jess heard footsteps, she perked up. Gumbo, friend to her now, lifted his head and gave a short deep bark of recognition. She put her hands to her head and shook her hair through them, rubbed the tear stains from beneath her eyes. She saw Dan, then she saw Lily behind him. Lily knew. Jess could tell. That was a shock. She had thought it would at least be 'their' secret. The only 'their'.

Lily came up to Jess. Dan stood behind her, like a schoolboy outside the headmaster's office, shuffling from one foot to the other. Then he said something: 'Leave you to it' – something like that. Jess felt herself growing cold towards him at the sight of his meek, retreating back.

'Will you have a cup of tea at my cottage, Jess?' Lily said.

And Jess said yes, because Lily was at least a person you could cry in front of.

When the tea is made: Lily says, 'It wouldn't have been Love.'

Jess looks at her, her lips pulled sullen. 'How would you know?' she says in the voice she uses on her mother from time to time. The tart, sharp voice of the pissed-off teen. It doesn't rile Lily though. Doesn't get the irritation rising in her like it does in her mum. Lily just gazes at her. As if, Jess thinks...as if she is about to cry herself. She looks so unhappy it quits Jess right out of her strop.

'I do know,' Lily says.

Jess, looking at her, hearing her, knows that she does. Although it is a limited knowing, framed as it is by her own experience, or lack of it.

'You're so lovely, Jess,' Lily says. Her voice almost cracks. 'Keep your lovely. Keep it all your own.'

The Layabout Boy, Jess's nemesis, had met a mate in town – weeks back now. On the way down King Street, 11:00

p.m., the mate had smashed the window of a parked car and grabbed a zip-up purse full of parking change from the compartment in the driver's side door. It was a beat-up car with a kiddie seat in the back – easy to rob, but slim pickings. The mate gave the car a kick before they legged it to the top of the alley where some dosser was set up for the night. They smoked a cigarette there and the Layabout Boy told his mate about the girl up at Motthoe – A Looker. Working in the garden. Been hoping to run into her some Friday in the town. Treat her to a couple, if you know what I mean. The mate knew what he meant. He laughed. Then he swore. Nothing, but sodding parking change. He chucked the purse and the remaining coins at the dosser. Laughed again. Then they took off looking for bigger fish.

Seth wasn't sure how he'd ended up in the town that night. He'd turned inward on the ring road at some point, into the scruffy side of the shopping centre, begged some cash from a young mum. She'd given it to him. They always did, the young mums, still sappy with love for humanity, reliable for a quid, or two if they had it – fossicking through those great canvas bags they always hung on the handles of the strollers, kids inside bundled like seals. The young mum had not looked directly at him. In that way she was the same as everyone else. People didn't look at him in case it was catchy – misery and degradation.

He was sat in an alley later, on a piece of card left by another man like him. A homeless, nameless man – a good man, a bad man, nobody distinguished, just a hollow-eyed, empty-headed scrap of a non-human being with nowhere to go and nothing to remember. Except that Seth did remember something. He remembered her. And when he had heard those two lads, who did not look his way, two lads talking of the fierce beauty gardening girl at Motthoe, he knew it was her and could picture her all over as if it had only been yesterday he'd last been with her, little Lily. Not so little, thirteen maybe. Old enough. She'd covered her tracks these last years. Still, now, he knew he'd found her again. Lily.

It was after one o'clock that night when he had set had off, on the road from town. Out the western side, water on the left, hills on the right. The road that led out over the bridge. Buildings had thinned and the cars, too. Headlights picked him out till he switched to the hilly side. Will o' the wisp, ghouly, dark in his clothes and his unwashed face. Hardly any teeth in his head to pick up the glare. He slunk against the grass when he heard an engine. No one saw him. No one cared. Out along he went – westwards. Out along the main road past the turn-off to the development where Irene's mother's bungalow sat cold now – damp setting in around the bottom of the window frame in the dull room that was once Irene's. The room she would never return to.

He had reached Motthoe just as Lord Harry of Dreams had welcomed one in – his always full of dare-deviling such as the days never showed him. Just as, on the floor below, Irene had turned on her curled side in the dressing room, clutching her phone to her chest ready for her lover's morning call. Just as Jess had twisted and lolled in her bedroom, shared with her sister who breathed deep three feet from her and Ruth, through the wall, had sat up and taken her wedding snap from the drawer in the bedside cabinet and then put it back again before the weeping took her. It was just as Irene's mother half woke and swung her feet out of the bed and toured the room, wondering where she was, then remembered and got back into bed. (She was at Motthoe, where she belonged. Where she'd always belonged – she'd known it as a girl, known it the first time she'd seen the music room, that this was the life she was meant for). As Dan had sat at his journal and recorded the day and added two paragraphs about carrots. As young Jason, far away, but at Motthoe in thought had wondered if Jess would ever notice him. As Ogden had said Goodnight to Mary and settled to brief sleep – he would be up for five. As all the night had dreamed and tossed and twisted and Lily had lain and slept thinly and not thought of her baby.

Seth had reached Motthoe that night in the graveyard hours – three, four – and wandered it undetected as carbon monoxide, and recognized the Lily Garden. And he had scoured the estate for a corner to live in and had found several. He had been living in them ever since. He'd been watching Lily ever since. Pregnant. Watching her dressing with her belly sticking out. It was by chance he'd come across that hat, waving on a bush on a path out back of the village, lost by some picnicking parent, but it was like he was meant to find it – a baby's hat. Somebody had stuck it there for somebody else to find. He'd found it, just as he had found her. Like he was meant to. He had put the kiddie's hat on her van door. She was a slut. But he still wanted her.

Harry counted the days after Lily's running away, and his fetching her back, the way a child counts those before

Christmas. She was going to have a baby. Maybe she loved the baby's father. Maybe the baby's father loved her. If that was true, he would not stand in their way. But if any part of it was not true, if there was any tendril of promise to which he could cling, he would cling fast to it, and advance along it – day by day, hour by hour, minute by minute, breath by breath until Lily saw that loving her was the one thing that Lord Harry of Hopelessness could do – would do perfectly.

CHAPTER TEN

Fitting that they should be sitting in Lily's garden; it had collected so many hearts. And tears.

'I'm generally better at writing things than saying them,' Dan said.

'Write them, then.'

He allowed himself to smile at her. 'No,' he said, 'that would be a letter and letters are a serious business.'

'I am serious,' Jess said. 'I'm not a kid, no matter what you think.'

'I don't think you're a kid,' Dan said. He had been clearing weeds for Lily when Jess had cornered him, blocked the path out under the wisteria. But, as it happened, he was quite willing to talk to her, to let her talk to him. The atmosphere between them had grown so brittle that other people were bound to notice, to recoil on walking into it. Jess had continued to watch him as earnestly as ever, but the looks she now sent him – flung with marksman accuracy – were as hard and sour as immature quinces.

'Frankness won't mend her heart,' Lily had said. 'But later she'll remember it and think of you less harshly.'

Dan had thought about that and eventually decided Lily was right. And that 'less harshly', even if suspended, was a state worth setting off for. But there are many men who will wait a while, a lifetime, until a woman comes along and tells them what to do, and Dan for the present had become one. He would never have opened the conversation with Jess himself.

He looked at her face now and almost sighed – it was still so transparent, still so clearly wavering between defiance and hurt and little-girl willingness. So young. So adorable and so young. Timing, he thought; cruel joker.

'You're not old,' Jess said. (All Defiance.)

'I didn't say I was,' he said, holding her eyes. 'I said you were very young. It's the in-between years that are wrong.'

'Some men wouldn't say that,' she countered.

'I know,' Dan said. 'And I hope you won't meet one of them.'

'What's that supposed to mean?'

'It means Jess that you are a beauteous thing, and not a kid, but a girl still and I wouldn't want anyone to take advantage of you.'

'You think you deserve a medal – for protecting me, or

something?'

'No, I don't think I've handled things in the least bit heroically. I just think you might change your mind soon and then you'd be sorry to be tied up with a guy like me. I know it would be wrong. I can't think of a gentler way to put it.'

She stared hard at him for a moment and then lowered her head and wept.

Dan wanted to extend his arms to her. He crossed them instead, and wished fervently that Lily would come through the arbor, in her big skirt, with her clippers in her hand and that serene, understanding look on her face. She didn't and he was sentenced to watching Jess and remembering that awful, bone-deep loneliness that the teenage years were riddled with for anyone intelligent, anyone different. Anyone who wanted more.

She lifted her helpless face to him and said, 'But I love you.'

Dan uncrossed his arms and put his hands in his pockets and met her eyes. 'I am not going to tell you what you feel Jess, but I don't think you know me well enough to come to any strong conclusions.'

'Well, I could say the same to you.' Jess knew that she was doing all the things you weren't supposed to do – Coming On Too Strong. She knew and she wished she could stop, but she couldn't. She felt as if everything had collapsed around her. As if Dan was her way back up. As if Dan's love could bring it all back...Her proper life, her father. But here he was ditching her just as surely as her father had. The tears continued to fall as she turned away from him and ran along the path through Lily's garden and into the woods.

Dan watched her go. Did not call out. Told himself she

would be fine. He got up and attacked a bindweed root and eventually tugged it free. Then he let himself think about how miserable Jess was and went to find Lily.

Lily listened.

'I've been going over it – whether I gave her any...'

'I know you've not encouraged her,' she said. A glance down, then back to his. 'And I know you've done right by her.' Steady-eyed.

Dan felt again the itchy prickle of some clue to Lily.

Irene is surprised by the affection she feels pulling the covers up over her napping mother. She sleeps afternoons now, hours and hours. She looks even older in sleep – the skin at her jaw pulled tight and her teeth too few in her head to give it shape. With the animation of her eyes gone, closed over, all her fire is out. Her fingers press at the bedding like the paws of a kneading kitten, and her head shakes gently against the white pillowslip. She looks harmless, worthy of protection. Irene berates herself for her years of mental railing. Time to let it go now, she thinks. She is just an old woman and the hurt is all gone.

She put the jug of water she had carried up on the bedside cabinet, but it almost tipped, the liquid angled across its surface. She picked the jug up again, to check for obstacles – pills, tissues, lozenges – underneath. There was a white cutwork doily on the cabinet, anchored by a lamp, she lifted its scalloped edge. Then she lifted the lamp, to examine what she had found there: a gold chain, a small bracelet, a locket, a key – from a music box, or some such – a tiny silver picture frame. In terms of value, the items were mixed. The locket, Irene thought, may have been an antique and had probably belonged to Harry's grandmother. Keys, though? None of them were worth anything to her mother. She had simply taken the things – reached out with the fingertips that were now unconsciously gnawing at an open-weave blanket – because they appealed to her.

Irene went to the corridor that divided her own dressing room sleeping quarters from her mother's room. There were cupboards there, lining the walls and she took from one her mother's dressing gown, and the long camel skirt with deep side pockets that she wore most often when she was up to wearing clothes. Irene found a corkscrew, another chain – possibly from a bathroom plug – and two more keys. Her mother had turned magpie, shine-thief.

Irene removed these spoils and went back to the kitchen where she was pleased to find Lily and Ruth, just Lily and Ruth. She held out her hands to them, filled with the bits and bobs.

'Jess's necklace,' Ruth said, leaning towards her and extracting the gold chain from the clutter. 'She's been in a state about that.'

'I am so sorry,' Irene said. 'I found this lot in my mother's room. She's been…taking things.'

'Serves Jess right for leaving it lying about. No harm done,' Ruth said.

Lily took one of the keys. 'I think this fits the trunk in the greenhouse,' she said.

'I had no idea,' Irene said.

'Don't worry,' Ruth said. 'She's old and her mind is playing tricks on her. That's all. No harm done,' she repeated.

'No, but...' Irene tucked a lock of her ever-softening hair behind her ear.

'Change,' said Lily. 'New surroundings can spark things in a person.'

'I know, and I know she's old,' Irene said. 'But I think – I just thought that when we came here, when we came here and I had help with looking after her at last, and she became so much more...malleable. Gentler. I thought we could heal a few things, I suppose, before...before it was too late. But if she's losing her marbles, that's not going to happen.'

'Oh, I don't know,' said Ruth. 'People tend to lose their marbles one at a time for a quite a while.'

'So, I've got a few months before they start rumbling away like turnips off a tractor,' Irene said.

She laughed. Ruth laughed. Lily laughed. Afternoon light flooding the kitchen. They all laughed until, outside, something spooked Gumbo, and he started to bark. He barked and would not let up barking. There was a deer maybe, too close to the house, something out of place. Then a scream – not a deer.

Lily jumped to the window, Ruth to the door. It was Callum who had screamed. He ran past, blind to everyone with his hands over his ears.

'Poor little chap – hates noise,' said Ruth.

Jason followed Callum – shouted out to him twice, though he knew it would do no good.

'Do you need help, love?' Ruth asked.

Jason shook his head, No, as he followed in his brother's frenzied little trail.

On the floor of the enormous airing cupboard, where it is quiet, dry and sweet smelling. There, in the cerement of lavendered air, in the three-foot space between the floor and the first shelf, crouches Jason, cap still on, long knees bent and feet planted and Callum, curled against him, rocking. Side to side. Side to side. Rocking in Jason's arms.

'*The owl and the pussycat*,' Jason croons, '*went to sea, in a beautiful pea green boat.*' Rocking and rocking. '*They took some honey*,' voice like velvet, steady as a metronome, '*and plenty of money.*' Rock…ing…rock…ing.

When Jess, wandering off her woes in the long, shadowed hallways and soothingly empty rooms, hears the mellifluous hum through the linen cupboard door, she understands not to open it, but she sits down and listens, leaning her back against the wall. Jason's voice is an adult, loving voice, as easing to her as it is to Callum. Hearing it she sees Jason for the first time. Which is timely, because Dan – who has escaped into town, clutching a ruse errand list – has just met the green gaze of a strong-minded, ukulele-playing, crop haired, gamine, thirty-year old brunette, from whom he has purchased a tub of black olives. She hands him his change. Her name is Meg, and she has always known that her One True Love would be a Scorpio.

Motthoe later: delicious with pleasantness, with peace, with understanding, with acceptance and caring, but Harry

is girded for the worst. He has embarked on The Rot
Tour with Irene's Nick. He expects any minute to hear –
reverberating through Motthoe like a gale – that sound.
The sound of air being sucked in between teeth, the sound
of derision and expense.

As they mount the stairs Harry remembers his father
walking the rooms and explaining them to him: talking
about the people who had dined and conversed and wed and
plotted and slept, and been born in them. The people who
had died in them. A prime minister's name and, in Harry's
great uncle's time, a prince. But these were the only nuggets
Harry recalled. His father's long lectures on the plaster work,
on the famous men's apprentices who had worked on the
drawing room, were forgotten. And, in any case, Harry didn't
altogether trust his father's versions, heavily steeped as they
always were in family glory. Harry had shunned the nonsense
cloak of pedigree, worn so tightly by some of the men in his
family, men who had clung to 'Squire'. Harry had never so
much as inked esq. after his name. Harry was Harry, lord of
nothing but dreams.

Now, shadowing Nick, Harry has several surprises. The
first is that Nick does not squint, snort, or lip-curl. Instead,
he inspects with an impassive face and undramatic eyes. He
is an engineer first, he tells Harry. He tends to think like
one – steady.

Nick, Harry thought, watching him, was something of
Lily's indoor equivalent. He looked through things the way
that Lily did, and seemed to understand what should go, what
should stay, what was of value – where life could be found
again. Harry was beginning to feel the way he had felt with

Lily that first day, as if shoots of possibility were springing through the cracks of his concreted-over life like daisies. His tread pepped up and his descriptions and his explanations became more enthusiastic, more voluble, as they moved from bedroom to bedroom, from bathroom to bathroom, and then back down – Harry's usual route – through the pantry and scullery and back to the music room, the library, the dining room…They finished in Harry's sitting room, just as Ruth came in with tea.

There was shortbread with the tea and Nick ate his slowly. He kept biting it and then looking at it, as if attempting to divine something from within. He drank his tea.

Harry watched him closely. Waiting. Wanting the news, but not wanting it.

'This shortbread is very, very good,' Nick said at last.

Harry was momentarily blindsided, but he rallied. 'Yes,' he said. 'Yes, Ruth bakes. The kitchen hasn't known so much activity since 1963.' He gave a laugh, horse-like and hollow. He was nervous, as if he were being judged, assessed. Get a hold of yourself, he thought, and rested back, deliberately against the sofa corner. He was in his own home after all. He forgot that sometimes.

Nick settled then too, his tea cup in his hand.

A decent man, Harry thought; honest, able, compassionate. And there was Irene, happy, and confident and prettier with joy by the day. A good story. Harry felt enlivened by it – as if happy endings might be infectious. Lily was still at Motthoe, if by a thread.

'I don't think it is as bad as it could be,' Nick said at last.

'No?'

'No,' Nick said. He smiled and helped himself to some more shortbread.

Harry let the grin splash all over him. First Lily and now Nick, how had he attracted these two, can-do souls? No matter. He had.

In the dry August garden, Lily looks up from staking her dahlias – they have grown heavy over their legs and blousy as she has – and she sees the fluffed stripes of an aircraft streaking the sky as if it is joining the clouds in a child's dot-to-dot picture. Strange, these reminders of the world outside Motthoe, which is now Lily's whole existence. She does not return Harry's love, but it steadies her in any case, emanating from him as it does, regular and constant as a lighthouse beam.

She is energetic in her pregnancy now, and has deadheaded and trimmed and cut back all week with spring zest. She has hand-mown the wildflowers herself and collected ripe seed. Bounty.

Dan is harvesting these long days, too: corn, beans. He is aware of the contentment that seeps through him at the sight of his crop. He walks over to help Lily most afternoons, prolonging the meaty healing of hands-on, fruitful work. He learns to make weed-killer from vinegar and salt, to use old newspapers for mulch. He listens when she instructs the household to save their washing water for the plants. He is in love with the productivity. Sometimes he is happy. He has had four pints of cider and three amiable conversations with Meg. She has made him laugh six times.

Irene and Nick and Harry come to the garden and begin discussing the lake – whether it would be better to refill, or fill it in. Insurance, says Nick. Kiddies, says Irene. And Nick, because he is at that stage of love where every warm moment plummets the lover further, smiles at her with such gentleness and depth that Harry, caught in it, feels a wave of love for Irene himself, and then he wanders off a bit, embarrassed.

Ogden, just out of sight, is fixing the top of a loose door slide in the greenhouse; pleased to be needed. Especially by Lily who has, by way of a sorry for her part in his misadventure in the hedge, replaced Mary's dead violets with new ones and set them in whitewashed pots on his porch – just as Mary might have done. Ogden had, coming home to see it, felt Mary's whole presence again, for the first time in a long time.

Now, atop his ladder he hears Irene's mother – in the chair they bring to the garden for her – singing: *There'll be bluebirds over...*

Callum's and Jason's mum, Sarah: Sees all of this, too. As does her husband, Doctor Galbraith. Harry has come to greet him, hugged Doctor Galbraith and his wife.

'It's good to see you,' says Harry. He means it.

'And you,' says the doctor. They played as children.

Both stand looking at each other for a moment, recognizing the nine-year-olds they were, remembering things: tree houses, long afternoons, sling shots. The doctor grins and then, in his haste to be helpful – Ruth is carrying a tray – turns to her. He is a man who is always helpful. His face rarely reflects the lack of advantages this trait has earned him.

Sarah saw all that was happening around her. But she saw it like a film, like a hologram, because the only thing that was real to her just then was Callum; Callum, chasing a butterfly, running, now along the pathway, now through the border, jumping from a low wall, laughing, holding out his dear hands, brushing past his big brother who patted his rushing head: take care buddy. Callum acknowledging this, grinning at Jason, his hands up again, for the butterfly. His mother lets her tears run down her face. Callum is nearly eight. Why hasn't he been this happy before?

Ruth knows. She smiles her Knowing at Callum's mother. It is Lily's garden. It casts a spell on people.

Ogden had caught the trout with live earthworm bait on the last rainy evening in July – up where the river narrows and kinks and the water goes from deep to shallow to deep. (He has taken his rod from the shed behind the porch that once housed Mary's bicycle twice in recent months and had a catch both times.)

Nick, at the head of the dining room table, his hair grazing his collar at the nape, his eyes happy as Irene's, tastes his trout and looks pleased. He turns to Lily: Would she expand the garden if she could – cut back the wood some and extend?

'No,' said Lily. 'If it were mine to say so. No, I wouldn't.'

Nick took another mouthful of trout before he moved his eyes to her again. 'Why not? I thought gardeners always wanted more ground.'

'Maybe,' she said, 'but I think this garden is already ideal.'

'Because of the proportions?'

'Yes,' Lily said. 'And the shape, the way it narrows at one end – it takes you on a journey.'

'In all directions,' Nick said.

'Yes,' Lily said. 'And you don't quite know where you will end up.'

'You have a real gift,' Nick said. 'I love to build things, but I deal more with absolutes. Of course, buildings change and you have to spend time thinking about that, construction has to combine the structural elements with design, but gardening…so many more unknowns. You have to do so much more on faith.' He put his fork down, turned almost square to her. 'I've seen the whole estate now and your corner of it is the truly living part, the most beautiful. That's talent. That's you.'

Lily felt the pinkness rise at her chest. 'I think,' she said, in a shy, but sincere diversion, 'that the kitchen might be going to put up some competition.'

After the trout, they ate partridge with Dan's kale and after the partridge, cherry pie – served straight from the enamel pie dish. Drips of gluey juice made stains on the table. There were bowls of cream from the farm.

It was late when they finished eating, midnight, thereabouts. Mildness had settled about the room like an eiderdown by the time Nick stood and unrolled a scroll of paper in front of him and weighted its upper corners with a pair of George VI napkin rings. He patted the paper in the center and began to speak. He had everyone's attention, but Irene did not hear what he said at first because the scent of him was so intoxicating. She imagined that every other woman there could smell it, too, and feel as giddy as she did.

'You could put a café here,' he said. He patted the paper again, and Dan and Harry tipped their heads leftward in unison. Nick looked at Ruth. 'That way you use the existing kitchen.'

Ruth nodded. She could see.

'You don't want to be spending money on developing or building outbuildings when the central structure is essentially sound,' Nick said.

Harry nodded.

'Where would folk sit? Where are the tables?' Ruth asked.

'Here,' Nick said. 'Here – you've got seating for forty, but then if you open the double doors here that go into the drawing room, you can extend it to around a hundred and fifty. I figure, that way you can use either one room, or both – for weddings and christenings and such, if you do those. Private parties, maybe. You already have the size. I think you might want to open up here on the side of the Aga and open out along where these rooms are, which are pretty much useless now – these store rooms – that forms a passage into here, so, again, you can use one room or both.'

He straightened up, heads around him were still bowed to his plans. 'The other option is not to do anything like this at all.'

Heads were raised.

'If you demolished the Victorian addition – here…which adds nothing to the building anyway, and made the rest of the roof completely watertight – you could live here…with enough people – enough of the right people – and be self-sufficient. The rents from the cottages, the sale of the land up river and a different sort of farming,' he looked at Ogden, who looked at him, embers of understanding catching between them. 'You wouldn't be aiming to create profit as such, but you'd do what Lily has done in her garden – make something wonderful that maintains itself.'

Nobody was ready to speak yet, and in any case, they would have all deferred to Harry, who was letting the heady amalgam of perspicacity and idealism seep through him, nice and slow.

'Motthoe could do that with careful management, I think,' Nick said. 'And an enthusiastic population – you've got that, almost…the beginning of it anyway, it seems to me. You need a few more people, of course. But it's got to be the Right People – it has to be people who see something here, people who want to make a life – a different life.'

At the end of the table, Sarah (who, along with Dr Galbraith, had been invited to supper while Ashley and Callum and Jason and Jess were let loose on a dozen sausages and a bottle of ketchup, and each other, in the kitchen) looked at her husband. She did not have to say: I hate working in Accounts at Gordon & Son – twenty-eight miles there and twenty-eight miles back, in traffic. Hours not child-friendly. No value in the pay any more. It didn't buy what she wanted. She had been subject to an epiphany, in the garden, that afternoon. This was what she wanted: to be near her children, while she still could be.

All right, said Doctor Galbraith, said Jason and Callum's father's eyes. If that is what you want, Sarah, I want it, too.

They were very happily married.

'You've got a good knowledge base between you,' Nick was saying. 'Cooking, gardening, administration, farming. You've got imagination (looking at Harry) and, if you're agreeable, (not looking at Irene) construction…'

'And accounting,' said Jason and Callum's mother.

'And medicine,' said her husband.

There was a rumble outside, the beginnings of a rainstorm, distant thunder. 1:00 a.m. – the heavens were re-aligning. Dan got up and stood next to Harry to look over Nick's notes with him, leaning in, he laid an arm across Harry's shoulders. It was if everyone in the room had held hands.

That night Lily let Harry walk her back to Ashcott. The storm had passed over but the air was still wet with it. Lily was too big now for the downhill of the field and they took the back road way.

'Do you want to check your plants before we leave?' Harry said before they turned toward the gate. It was a question that Lily loved him for.

'No,' she said. 'But thank you for thinking of it.'

'I remember how worried you were – in that last thunderstorm.'

'Yes,' she said. 'I was. But I don't worry so much anymore.'

'Good,' he said. Inside him, one more little Hope Brick was added to his building assurance.

CHAPTER ELEVEN

L ily stirred and shivered. She got up, pulled her cardigan around her shoulders and went downstairs. She opened the stove door with a cloth over her hand. The ash was thick on top. She prodded at it with the poker so that it fell through the grate to the tray below. When the glowing cinders were exposed, she took some kindling from the basketful she'd collected in the woods – dry twigs, snapped into roughly even lengths. She dropped them in and watched them catch. Then she put on a small log – Ogden had sawn them for her and left them at the kitchen door. When the fire flickered, she added a second log and built it to a roar, then she shoveled on some charcoal and closed the door again. A luxury, a big fire on a September morning. Her days were all-over luxurious now, great fattening days of love and succor.

She drank her tea with both hands on the cup and watched the mist up on the rise of hill behind the cottage burning off, sky beneath it as blue as the ocean, as blue as the sky. Puffs of white cloud and a skidding wind, the tops of the field grass moving gently. Buttercups, heartsease. A perfect day for blackberrying.

It was Saturday morning; the big house was sleeping late. Except for Irene's mother who rose, and wandered, oatcakes in her pocket from the plate Irene had left beside her bed in case of night-wakings. She peeped out of a landing window and saw Lily come up by the back door to fetch a basket, but Lily did not see her. Watching Lily walking off alone with the basket swinging, she remembered something. Blackberries! She remembered picking them. She wanted to call out to the girl, the girl with the baby coming on, to take care. Blackberries, she remembered this too, tempted a person; up one more hill, along one more lane. The fattest ones were always just out of reach. She thought Lily ought to have a companion. But she only thought it, and said nothing. And then she thought of something else. Her head was always full of things; thoughts, ideas, all knotted together, but tangled like string in a drawer. She fetched out one of her pocket oatcakes and tipped her head, peering at it like a sparrow, wondering how it had got there.

Lily set off, up the back track through the woods, through the enchanted morning, alone. Her baby inside her felt solid and reassuring, felt like a baby, Lily could imagine walking this path with her baby strapped at her chest.

The track was flat and no strain for Lily, who was in any case fit and strong, her legs as slim as they had been before her pregnancy which was, Jason and Callum's Dad had assured her, doing nicely. Very nicely indeed. Lily had wondered looking at his smile; had Callum's birth been a normal one, had there been any sign then, that Callum would be...Callum? Different, special. She wondered about her own child and whether those sorts of differences would daunt her. No, she decided, not now, nothing would now. Her dauntings were laid to rest with the acceptance, finally, the proper acceptance of the new life before her.

The lane was alive with squirrels and bees and birds who knew (no matter the human tendency to elongate summer if they can, to idle through a sunny September as if it were July) that it was time for organizing, preparing, reaping. Now Lily would join them.

She didn't bother with the parched first fruit she found, but continued up the hill and took the stile into a second wooded path and then came out the other side into a clear field. There was a bank on one side and she crossed the open grass expanse feeling the joy of it and her bigness and the sun on her arms and her wellness and the happiness of Motthoe life, and she clambered the bank and began to pick her way along it. She had a bottle of water with her and stopped when the bucket was half full to sit and drink it. The grass was damp through her skirt. Behind her a chaffinch darted in and out of the hedge.

She got up again and filled the basket to almost three-quarters, and, turning to come back down the hill, slipped. She came down sideways just as a wheel of crows and rooks rose from a distant oak in a cloud and circled the field. They shrilled and cawed above her until, as at some signal they returned to the tree and re-blackened its branches.

Lily was a little shaken by her fall. And her ankle was hurt, but, testing it, she felt she could manage, could get home. The decision was whether to leave the blackberries. She could hobble without them. If she could get to the wood, she would find a stick, and then she would be fine. A lot of the blackberries had scattered and she felt saddened by that. A small loss, and yet it had punctured her mood and then: her heart began to beat hard and she felt the familiar inner rise of the old panics.

Lily twisted her head about, one side to the other, taking stock, and saw nothing, nothing save the scene that had afforded her such pleasure only half an hour before. But it had changed. She knew that it had changed. And she was right, and she knew she was right, because it was then that Seth decided to show himself to her.

He looked frail, pitiable if you weren't Lily. Thin, teeth missing. His skin drawn over his cheeks so that his skull showed through – cadaverous. His khaki coat was too big for him and drooped from his shoulders which hunched. He had a knapsack slung over one of them and in his opposite hand a tall stick – willow maybe, a hedgerow stick. His long hand was wrapped around it. His eyes, though sunken, were the same. The line of his mouth had changed completely, from the missing teeth probably, and he was no longer handsome. And, despite the eyes, you could not see that he ever had been. But he had. He had been very handsome. Hadn't the girls at school, the girls she'd known for that short while when things had seemed heavenly, all swooned? That short while when her mother had found the perfect bloke and been home when Lily got off the bus more often than she was not. That while, when things had been looking up for the two of them at last – when Lily was thirteen. When Seth had come along. Things had been great. 'That your dad then?' the girls had asked. 'Mum's boyfriend,' Lily had corrected. But even at that age, half-grown, so much life already behind her, she had allowed herself to imagine Seth as her dad. He did things that dads did. Helped out. Hugged her mum. Hugged her. Teased her. Life had been on the up. Seth, a handsome Dad of her own. At last.

'Hello, Lil?' he said. She didn't answer. Another day it might have made her jump. Not today, she sat where she was, with her ankle swelling and her teeming insides swish swishing like a washing machine and the rest of her frozen. Like the world suddenly was. She had stopped breathing. All was dead. She was dead. Because if Seth touched her, she would die. She had always known that. All these years on the run from the phantom. Not a phantom at all.

'I expect you thought I was dead,' Seth said, and this word woke her. She went from petrified to rattlesnake heedful. Her eyes remained fixed on him, but her brain began to race. Running? Couldn't. Screaming? She tried it. Nothing came out. Her lips in fact did not move. It was like one of those stories you read, about people being awake during an operation. She was awake, but she could not move. She stared.

'I did my time, Lily,' he said, coming nearer. 'And a bit

more time after that. Then I went on the streets. It was hard, Lil. I've had it pretty hard.'

He said this as if – what? As if she might feel that he had made up for things, paid his dues. Her voice, came up, deep and real, sepulchral, from far down inside of her.

'Stay away from me.' Gaps between the words. Each weighted.

Seth held his free hand up, signaling truce, but at the same time took another step…nearer.

'I love you, Lily. That was all that kept me going. Through all these bad times. Hard, hard times. I loved you and I looked for you and I followed you and that's what kept me going. Just seeing you was enough. Meat and drink to me. But now, today, it was like a voice in my head, the sun, and you so beautiful with your baby coming and I knew today was the day.'

Ice dripped down Lily's spine. He had been watching her. Every minute of every joyful day over the past months was tainted. She felt revulsion and horror. The scream came then. High as a poplar, up and over, and carrying off with the wind which was blowing today north east, away from Motthoe. No one would hear her and she would die in the hedgerow along with her baby.

Seth, at the scream, rushed her and felled her and they lay side by side, hearts crashing. He looked completely different, but his hand over her mouth felt exactly the same.

'You don't know, Lily,' he said, in a whisper so throatily intimate that it made her retch. 'There's been times when I've honest to God wondered if any voice at all would come out if I tried to speak. That was how long I went not speaking. Not speaking to a living soul, Lil. Just me on the road, nothing but the sound of my own footsteps and my thoughts in my head. Thoughts going round and around in my head, Lil. Mostly of you. You were the best thing I had to think about. The best thing, Lily. Do you hear that, you were the best thing in my life? My whole shithole life. You always were.'

He moved, edged sideways. Lily, who was still lying on her back, felt his hand loosen and, simultaneously, her bile rise. She half sat on reflex to prevent herself from choking. Seth draw-ready again, held his head and eyes to her. No distance between her face and his, he pulled her up and forward, bent her without removing his hand. The other hand was behind her head, the palm flat there. Then he took both hands off her as she vomited, into the grass, into the red clover, stalwart little flower, beside her.

When she raised her head again, he left her mouth uncovered – a small blessing with which she could make no hay. All energy, all effort was gone from her. He could see it. Her eyes were voids.

'I had all these years, thinking of what to say and now I can't say it,' he said.

He half-smiled at her. It was a look that a boy might give a girl on a date. A shy boy, a sweet girl. A pair of soon-to-be lovers. Lily was repulsed. Cold settled on her gut. Even the baby was still. She put her fingers to her belly, one arm across herself, her knees drawn up. She could feel the grass underneath her and smell her own vomit and the foul odor of him, but these things were outside her. She was observing herself.

'I believed you were dead,' she said, looking out beyond at

the still lovely meadow. 'I believed it, but I didn't think it. It was like a superstition. I thought…if I kept an eye out, didn't accept that you were dead, that you would be…'

'Don't start screaming again,' he said with low menace. His position mirrored hers, knees up, arms ready.

'Nobody would hear me,' she said.

He looked around as if checking the veracity of this and was met with nothing but sky and trees and grass.

'They never did,' she finished.

She felt the agitation flood him. He would surely kill her now. She assumed that was what he had come for. She put both arms across her unborn child and lowered her head.

'Fuck,' he said. 'This is…It's all fucked up. I didn't…'

That was when they heard the shout. Ogden. Way off, not visible, shouting at his dog. Seth grabbed Lily's arm and dragged her on her back towards the hedge and she screamed again. He elbowed her hard for it, but it didn't matter. She pulled back and twisted around and kicked up at him at him with one good foot. His left fist balled and raised. Her still prone, but she was fighting at last, fighting for her baby, and knowing, too, in the part of her that knew anything, that she was, at the same time, putting her baby's life at risk, putting both their lives at risk.

Seth pulled her to her feet, some notion of carting her off – where? – apparently firming in his head. 'This is all fucked up,' he shouted. He was working to some plan – concocted over years and now disintegrating, some impossible hypothesis.

He wrenched her by the hand, and she wrenched back and separated them and staggered backwards – it was then, when they were at their widest point apart, that the shot boomed and he fell.

Lily fell, too, rolling sideways.

Seth pitched backward into the hedge, his hands flying out either side of him, crucified there – head blasted backward by the impact.

Lily spun her attention to Seth first; to the killed, not the killer. He did not seem dead. He had been shot in the eye. His body twitched, slumped, the whole of him slid down, scratching against twigs, then he stopped, a small branch hitching his coat and preventing him just from reaching the ground. Lily's heart stopped, she expected him to halt his downward progression and stand and turn and grab her again, but he did not. He hung there, breathless as she was, looking like a scarecrow, stuffed with straw and dressed in rags.

There was silence as there only can be after a sound that shakes the world. But then there wasn't; the distant thrum of Ogden's plowing further up the valley, water splashing over stones in the stream, the fluty trill of a Mistle Thrush.

Lily took her eyes from the body beside her and looked towards the copse – fifteen-twenty yards off, four or five trees, plenty to hide a very small person. She was leaning against a beech trunk, the shotgun broken over her elbow. She wasn't looking at Lily, who limped as fast as she was able towards her now.

'I got him, didn't I?' She smiled.

'Yes,' said Lily. She did not smile back, but reached and took the gun and leaned it on a tree.

'I got him.'

Lily nodded and took the old lady's two arms with her own shaking hands.

'You must be on your guard all the time,' the old lady said.

Irene's mother dipped her head and swished it so that the look of a little girl took over her. She clutched at Lily. '*All* the time.' Her expression now that of a serious six-year-old. She told Lily, 'You should not have come out alone. It's not safe in war time.'

Lily nodded again, firming her hands on the thin elbows, though the old lady seemed less physically exhausted than she was. Now, Lily's entire body was struck by a shudder that hit her at the head and rippled to her knees.

'We need to go back to the house,' Lily said. With effort, gargantuan effort, she pulled herself in, held herself upright. She flicked her eyes back to the dead man in the hedge. 'We need to tell someone.'

'Yes. We need to tell someone we've killed one,' said Irene's mother, doe-eyes wide with triumph. 'A filthy Nazi.'

She never once varied in her description of the soldier she had seen grab Lily. She expected, she said, that they would find his parachute nearby. He must have been dropped. A spy.

Where had she found the gun? In the cabinet, locked, in the office. She'd seen them put it there. Seen young Harry hide the key. You could manage these things if you were smart. Smart and quiet. She was smart and quiet. You had always to be on the lookout. Always. Couldn't let your guard drop in war time, she said. Soon she had stopped making sense at all.

Ogden had heard the shot; thought it was Dan, he said – out for a duck, or a moor hen. Dan, looking for rabbits for supper. It was only when he'd turned the tractor and the blasted dog had taken off again that he'd seen Lily and the old lady, holding each other up – like the old lady was poorly, or Lily was. He couldn't see and the dog was yammering the whole while. Anyhow, he'd swung down and come after the dog and found the body. Not pretty, not even before the shot had been fired. A tramp. Like the tramps they used to get in the old days, in his boyhood, in the lanes – wandering the lanes and living out. The old tramps. This one smelled bad. Front of his face was gone, right side. Shot off. That was when he'd put two and two together and come up to the house. Found the old lady gabbling and Lily white as a sheet and as flappy as one on laundry day, ready to pass out. He'd yelled for Ruth, upstairs with the Hoover, and Irene had come out of her shower and Harry had run downstairs. Then Dan at the door. Lily all this while saying nothing.

Ruth got her to sit down, in the end. Irene dealing with her mother. The mother thought she'd shot a spy. Kept calling her daughter by some wrong name. Called Harry *sir*. Thought she'd shot a German soldier. Thought she was back in the war.

Dan had gone to fetch the gun.

Harry walked to the strip of grass near the copse and set down his tools. He faced north and paced out a rectangle, six foot five by three feet. He did not begin to dig immediately as he might have done, but instead pegged the corners of the area and ran some of Lily's gardening twine to each of the pegs. He checked the lines and measured off with a retractable measure – zipping it back into the palm of his hand as assuredly as any contractor might, as assuredly as Nick would have.

Nick had advised him on the technical details; shoring, sloping the sides, and Harry had taken close note, been intent on every word at the meeting they had held – Harry, Dan, Nick, Irene, Ruth. They had voted and no-one had hesitated. This is the right thing, said Ogden with paternal seniority. And they all believed, had faith that it was. The surprise had been Harry's insistence that he would take on this part of the job alone, the part that fitted more naturally with the other men there – the men whose hands habitually overtook Harry's in these sorts of tasks. But Harry had known it was his to do – on his land. And his love that should fuel the digging. He had not had to repeat his claim. Ogden had patted him between the shoulders and said, 'Do what you think is best, son.'

The gods had been kind and sent a night of benevolent rains to make the job easier. Soft wet had run into, rather than off the ground, and, at this lower end of the field, the first two feet of digging would present no problems. Harry, though, did not begin to dig immediately, he was heeding the inner call for precision, for exactness, for preparation.

Once the lines were marked, he stepped to the center of the left hand one, faced out and took two paces, like a parading soldier. He marked a second line, parallel, using the edge of his spade. He did the same on the right side. After that he lifted and set aside the top six inches of turf, in twenty-by-twenty-inch sections – neat as jigsaw pieces.

When that was done, he began to dig at the outer lines – left side then right. He dug one spade depth down, two spade widths in, shelving.

When he was two shelves down, he took the first strike straight down at the center trench, pummeling into the soil all his love for Lily, all the rage of his pain for her. Over and over, she had told him. Seth had hurt Lily, over and over, when she was young, when she was a child. She had said it with such stillness that he had momentarily feared for her sanity – her perfect face (the scratch marks on it vermillion to Harry) was stone.

They had brought her to Harry's bedroom – the most inhabited and least dank, other than Irene's mother's. That's where Lily had done her telling. While Ruth had made pot after pot of tea. Dan had argued for brandy, but Harry said, 'No, Lily is expecting a baby. She doesn't drink,' and Dan had acquiesced – it wasn't a moment for division.

Harry had held the tea to Lily's lips and she had sipped once or twice before her eyes rolled upward and fixed on the acanthus scroll of the cornicing.

She had told her mother, she said – said it so quietly that Harry had to lean his ear almost to her bruised mouth.

'I told my mother,' she said. 'When I was sixteen. Seth had been gone by then for almost three years, but he was still with us every day to me.' Tiny, tiny voiced. 'I told her.'

'Yes,' said Harry, trying to match her volume, feeling his intestines constrict with the repression of his own anguish, wanting to reassure, to tranquilize, be everything she needed.

She dropped her eyes to him, seeing him. It gave him strength. 'Yes,' he said again.

'She didn't answer,' Lily said. 'She didn't speak at all. She went on with what she was doing – reading about some movie star in a newspaper. She went on reading as if I hadn't said anything.'

Harry waited. He was beside her on the bed. He rolled onto his side so as to watch her. To watch her breathe. To live her every moment with her.

'And the strange thing was that I began to believe that I hadn't. I began to believe that the words had only come out in my head. I went away very soon after that and I hardly ever saw her again. It was only when she was dying, the night she died, that I really knew – I knew that I *had* told her.'

Harry put his right hand on her right forearm. It was lying, as if unattached to her, motionless between them. Her skin was the skin of an apricot, his stroke gossamer enough not to disturb its down.

'And I knew that she had heard me,' Lily said.

Harry had put his arms around her then and been relieved to hear the first sob, the first mourning. She had fallen asleep in his arms eventually, curled against him so that the swift, athletic push of the baby's foot from her insides had struck him in his; igniting an instant, unbreakable bond between them.

She had woken this morning, turned her head to him and smiled.

Now Harry struck the spade into the ground, pummeling into the soil all his love for Lily, all the rage of his pain for her.

The nature of Harry's assignment might have been apparent from the air, a raven might have understood his objective, but from all other viewpoints it would have been a matter of guesswork and, even the airborne would have a complete view obscured by the waving line of beeches and the soft foliage that still clung to them. Harry dug, thup-thup with the spade, high and wide, sleeves rolled to his elbows, boots to his knees. And he dug. By 3:00 p.m. he had reached the substrata of soil where the earth began to compact, but he worked at the same even pace, neatly cutting down with his spade so that the edges of the whole were straight and clean. And he dug. At four he stopped and drank the flask of tea that Ruth had packed in a wicker picnic basket covered with a tea cloth, and he ate the sandwiches she'd sent – ham with mustard. Irene had put fruitcake in for strength and remembered paper napkins. He used one to wipe his brow and then, rested, he set about it again. And he dug.

The days were drawing in, mid-September – afternoons like summer, but the bite of autumn in the dawn and dusk. He felt, by five, quite cool, though the work was getting harder, he had reached the rocky layer. Images came to his mind from geology lessons at school. He let them in because at 5:15 he was assailed by a picture of Lily as a terrified thirteen-year-old and it was an image he wanted to banish for ever. He struck the earth with such violence that the spade might have broken, but it did not. Thup, thup. Mechanical, methodical, anesthetic. He dug, down and down.

He went to five foot – it is a myth that people are buried six feet under, Nick had said, five foot would do it. He shored the central trench with strip of plywood at either end, unnecessarily, for his own peace of mind only – he had done the thing right, absolutely right – and he pulled out. He sat on the edge of the pit for a moment, looking in, breathing hard, feeling the sweat on his forehead and behind his ears

Deborah McKinlay

and his neck. It was dark.

He had a lantern. He set it on the ground, put aside the tools, wrapped them again in an old towel and left them under the trees, lifted the lantern and trekked, cross country to Ogden's cottage where it had been agreed they would meet: Ogden, Nick, Dan and Harry.

They carried Seth's body from Ogden's freezer to the tractor and began the transport, Seth's final wander of the hedgerows, at midnight. They lowered him, wrapped in an embossed banqueting cloth, into Harry's trench and the four of them took turns shoveling the soil back in. Nick and Dan laid the turf slices back across the top. Falling leaves would cover them soon, and the rains and winds of autumn would move the soil and plants to fill the seams. When it was done, they stood a moment. No one leading an exit.

Harry, understanding the need for ritual in even the least lamented of deaths, closed his eyes and incanted, '*Quia in inferno nulla est redemptio, miserere mei, Deus, et salva me.*' over what was now, unequivocally, a grave.

They exhaled as one and turned away. It was over. At least this part was. They would live with the rest for ever.

In the two weeks that it took for her to die from pneumonia, Irene's mother did not say any of the things that Irene longed to hear. Irene could not have specified exactly what these things were, but she could imagine the bounteous, fulfiling flavour of them perfectly: Motherly things. Apologetic things even. The sorts of things, the sorts of words that

252

Irene could revisit after her mother had gone, the way some people handle a piece of jewelry, or clothing left by a loved one – the whisper of the departed still in them. She wanted some words that she could recall as she put a small, familiar object, something her mother had owned and touched, in a keeping spot. Words she would think of when she looked at this thing in years to come. Words that would erase the years before they had been said.

But Irene's mother did no such thing. Irene nursed her diligently as she always had, dozing in the chair beside her, though other people – Ruth, Lily – offered to relieve her. It was her duty. She was the daughter and she had done her duty by her mother always. Nick marveled at Irene's devotedness. He decided to ask her to marry him, but Irene, unaware of this Eden in her way, of the great joys ahead, still sought unction from her mother's lips. Sometimes, in the night, her mother mumbled and Irene snapped up, reached out and said, 'Yes, Mother,' but the mumbling never took shape.

The doctor came – Jason's father, Callum's father, Doctor Galbraith, beginning his weave into Motthoe now (house up for sale) – and told Irene that her mother really ought to be in hospital, but then he looked at her, in her pristine bed, comfortable and calm and said that perhaps they'd wait another day, as long as she was being nursed so well – to call him if there was the slightest change, the slightest deterioration. Irene assured him that she would. Her mother, in the moments when she was awake, taking one sip of broth from a cupful, gave her frightened looks. Irene took them to mean that she did not wish to die in the hospital. It was a wish her mother had apprised her of many times when she was very far from dying. Irene intended to make it come true.

Once, in the course of that last illness, Irene's mother reached her hand out to Irene and laid it on top of hers. They both looked down at her knuckles as if surprised by this development – Irene waited. The old lady, rallied, almost righted herself and said…'Water'. It was a disappointment, but Irene was of such forbearing character that she took this anyway, this moment of contact, of physical warmth between them, as something – some sort of corroboration that they had not always got on, but that her mother understood some things about her, that her mother wished her well.

In fact, this would have been enough for Irene – her expectations were never great, having never been given any growing room – except that, one evening, she finally accepted one of Lily's offers to sit at her mother's bedside awhile, so that she could take a bath. Lily's bruises were hard to say no to, and Irene suspected that she needed employment, too, given what she had been through and the limiting aspects of her late pregnancy in terms of gardening. She hurried the bath and returned and heard through the ajar door of her mother's bedroom, Lily and her mother in full and earnest conversation – though her mother's voice was rasping with the effort. Irene could not make out what they were saying, and was not likely in any case to snoop, but nevertheless, the conversation was clearly heartfelt. Two voices, back and forth, a beat that her own conversations with her mother had never attained, a flow between the speakers as if they understood one another. She stood in the hallway with her damp hair, feeling its chill against her scalp, listening to the voices rise and fall.

It had made her want to cry. She had gone in before she had. Lily had been holding her mother's hands. It was a hard concession for Irene – that her mother was, could be in fact, loved, could engender such positive feelings in others. It meant that the fault, at least in part, must be hers.

Lily, turning to Irene, looked at her, and Irene consoled herself with the thought that it was Lily, after all. The Lily Effect; affection, like the scent of jasmine, hovered about her. Lily, leaving one hand on Irene's mother's hands, reached out to hold one of Irene's own, so that they were linked, the three of them, so that Irene's mother's last warmth could flow through her to Irene. Lily, the conductor of love.

Lily's baby: born a week after Irene's mother's gentle funeral. Born among the asters. She is fat and dark and delivered in the yellow bedroom – chosen by Lily, readied by Irene and Ruth. Lily names her daughter Eden. Harry lifts Eden in her first minute of life and vows to let her choose her own way, to burden her with nothing, and then he looks at Lily over the sweet head and makes the same promise to her.

CHAPTER TWELVE

Christmas Eve: He had walked the driveway, as Lily once had, as Harry once had – parked in the layby below and smoked a cigarette out of pure nerves. He'd given up smoking really, Ruth didn't like him smoking and he'd given up. Expensive habit in any case. He was being frugal – had to be, with Ruth gone. He sat in the car and smoked slowly, with the door open so as to let the cold wind off the water wash away some of the smell. Some of his fear. After the cigarette, he wiped his hands on his hips and brushed his hair again with his palms and sucked on a peppermint. In all, it was thirty-five minutes he was there plucking up courage, and for ten of those he still wasn't sure he would do it. Would go up there and see her, and his daughters.

He got out of the car, shut the door and locked it, and set off up the hill of the house approach, one hand in his pocket and a bunch of flowers in the other. The flowers were for Ruth: yellow daisies like he'd brought her the first time he took her out. They'd been walking along the street and he'd lifted the daisies from a bucket-full outside a florist, the stems had dripped. After that he'd brought them for her on anniversaries. For all those years. He'd had a job to find daisies today, in December, but he had. They were good years, his and Ruth's years. Too good to throw away.

Ruth's husband climbs the hill as the snow, which has been promised all day, the snow which has depressed the sky, but excited the anticipations of those who live under it, begins to fall. It is dark and the subduing of the atmosphere that the snow will complete by dawn has begun. All sound is muffled. The toll of the church bell calling the faithful (numbering approximately four) and the not-so-faithful, but yule-sprit filled, to the carol service travels to Motthoe heavily, thick and rounded as if sifted of its sharps by the flakes.

Inside, those who live there now: Harry, Lily, baby Edie, Dan, Ruth and Jess and Ashley, Jason, Callum, and their parents, Irene and Nick are pulling on their coats and boots and scarves and hats (along with Meg and Ogden, who have come up for eggnog and tree-trimming). Harry is singing: *O come ye, O co-ome ye to Be-ethlehem.* They will be late. They will stand at the back. The service will be better attended than any other service of the year – the church being too outlying even to attract city brides on the hunt for bucolic backdrops for their photographs.

The snow falls and the bell tolls.

It tolls over Seth. Where, beneath the snow, wild cyclamen corms are establishing themselves. They will be blooming when Lily walks to the beech copse with her child, early spring, March first, to put him to rest as far as she is able. And to remind herself of the fathomless love of her husband.

Glossary

Literary References

"Minnehaha, Indian maid and legendary beauty." As depicted in 'The Song of Hiawatha' by H. W. Longfellow

"In that rich earth a richer dust concealed" From 'The Soldier' by Rupert Brooke

"Had I the heavens embroidered cloths, Enwrought with golden and silver light…" From 'Cloths of Heaven' by William Butler Yeats

"And all that's best of dark and bright" From 'She Walks in Beauty' by Lord Byron

"The owl and the pussycat went to sea, in a beautiful pea green boat. They took some honey…" From 'The Owl and the Pussycat' by Edward Lear

"Quia in inferno nulla est redemptio, miserere mei, Deus, et salva me." Translation from Latin: For there is no redemption in Hell, have mercy on me, O God, and save me (Office of The Dead, prayer cycle, third matins, Catholic and Anglican churches)

About the Author

Deborah McKinlay is the author of two previous novels, *The View From Here* and *That Part Was True*. She lives and writes in the west of England.